LARS

SHIFTER ROMANTIC SUSPENSE

ANN GIMPEL

Edited by
ANGELA KELLY
Illustrated by
FIONA JAYDE

CONTENTS

LARS

~

Rubicon International, Book Two
by
Ann Gimpel
Undercover Shifter Bad Boys = Alphas With Serious Attitude

Tumble Across the Rubicon Into the Death-Riddled World of
International Espionage

BIRTH OF RUBICON INTERNATIONAL

This next section also prefaced *Garen*, book one of the Rubicon International series. If you've read that book, you can return to the table of contents and skip right to Chapter One of *Lars*.

CROSSING the Rubicon is an expression that means taking an irrevocable step, casting the dice, and being willing to live with the consequences.

BOSTON HARBOR
September, 1773

"YOU CAN COME OUT NOW."

Garen pounded a fist on the cabin Lars had barricaded himself into a few hours after their ship sailed out of Marseille's harbor four weeks before. They'd run into a spate of rough weather, or they'd have made Boston a week earlier.

Garen knocked again, louder this time although as a mountain cat shifter, Lars had exceptionally keen hearing.

"Stop!" Lars' heavily accented voice growled from beyond the door. Moments later, it flew open.

Garen fell back a pace. His friend was noticeably lighter, and his face held a haggard aspect. "Christ, you look like hell. I know you didn't leave your cabin much, but didn't the crew bring you food?"

A gurgling snort rippled past Lars' lips. "What for? I would just have heaved it back up. I ate, but not much."

Garen gazed about the cabin. "Looks like you're ready to leave."

Lars didn't answer. Just moved his collection of valises, crates, and leather bags toward the door. "I have been *ready to leave* for weeks. I will need a day or two to recover."

Privately, Garen thought he'd need longer than that, but shifters had decent recuperative powers. Much more efficient than their human counterparts.

"Where are your things?" Lars gathered his long, white-blonde hair in both hands and tied a leather thong around it, binding it into a thick queue that hung down his back.

"I hired a lackey. He'll be around any moment for your luggage. A carriage on the docks will take us into town."

Lars squeezed his gray eyes shut for a moment. "I cannot begin to describe how anxious I am to get off this ship." He dropped into shifter mind speech. *"Cats were never meant to travel over water."*

Garen punched him in the arm. "Maybe not."

"Remind me why you dragged us across the Atlantic."

Garen frowned. "Why? You already know."

"Humor me, old friend."

"Simple enough. The chaotic political environment in Europe and—" Garen switched to telepathy *"—that lucrative job offer spying for the newly formed American Colonies."*

"Thank you for indulging me. I needed to hear the *lucrative* part again. It does not exactly make up for how miserable I was, but—"

Lars broke off abruptly when the shaggy, smelly man Garen had hired to transport their luggage trotted into view.

"These things?" He pointed at the collection of bags and raised rheumy, brown eyes to peer at Lars. "Rough for you, eh? Some folk, they never get sea legs."

Garen cleared his throat. "Sooner you get our things moved to the carriage, sooner you'll get paid."

"Yeah, yeah. You hired my back, not my tongue." The man blew out onion-saturated breath and loaded Lars' items onto a wheeled cart he dragged behind him. Greasy, dark hair hung around his face, and his clothing had more patches than original fabric. Despite the chill weather, he was barefoot.

Once he left, whistling a tuneless song, Lars leaned closer to Garen. "Apparently the New World has not treated everyone well."

"Neither did the one we left." Garen cast an appraising glance his way. "You weren't planning to stay on this side of the Atlantic. Did the ocean crossing change your mind?"

A ghost of a smile lightened Lars' even features, but didn't quite make it to his eyes. "I came along for the adventure aspect—and got a bit more than I bargained for."

"Will you go back to Germany?" Garen led the way around the ship's deck to a rickety gangplank.

"*Ja.* Not for many months, though."

"Maybe by then, they'll have invented a more stable ship."

"Ha! Very funny."

Garen extended an arm. "The black carriage is ours."

"If town is not far, we should walk for many reasons. It will give us information and allow us—or me—to recover faster."

"Good idea. Annoyed I didn't think of it first." Garen trotted to the carriage. He paid the lackey and gave more money to the driver with instructions to leave their things at Newport House.

Lars had already started off at a reasonably brisk pace, considering how beaten down he'd looked in his cabin. Garen ran to catch up. He eyed thick timber on both sides of the deeply rutted dirt track leading into Boston. His wolf was close to the surface. Anxious to run free after the claustrophobic ship.

"What would you think about—?"

"Not a good idea." Lars cut in, casting a sidelong glance his way. "It is an obvious suggestion. I would love to take my other form, but for that we need night and a location farther from human habitation."

"No one looks twice at us throughout Europe," Garen pointed out.

"True enough, but until we understand the lay of things here, it pays to be careful. Our kind are hunted through the Ottoman Empire."

Breath puffed through Garen's teeth, making clouds in the chill air. Of the two of them, Lars was the cautious one, and the more levelheaded.

"We were late arriving," Lars continued. "You missed your assignation by at least three days."

"They'll find me." Garen felt confident his employers would know his ship had finally docked.

A musket ball whistled through the air, distressingly close. Cursing in German, Lars zigged and zagged a path into huge evergreens with Garen close behind. Arrows followed, along with more rifle fire and a bevy of outraged shouts.

"What the hell?" Garen ducked behind a thick tree bole, shoving thick black hair out of his eyes.

"Arrows must mean the native dwellers on this land are unhappy about something." Lars shook his head. "Perhaps sending the carriage away was a hasty decision."

Peering through tree branches, Garen noted that other foot traffic on the road hadn't cleared out. Perhaps such things were commonplace here. He twisted his face into a grimace. "It appears we overreacted."

"I came to the same conclusion." Lars flexed fingers with claws extruding from the ends. They vanished quickly, but his control over his animal form was usually better than that.

Garen snorted. "My wolf's not happy, either. Let's hurry into town. We're bound to make a mistake or two. Neither of us knows anything about the American Colonies."

"We must learn, and damned fast," Lars muttered.

"You're better?" Garen eyed him closely.

"Having your feet on ground that's not pitching, heaving, and rolling would make anyone *better*." Still grumbling, Lars plodded back toward the road.

Garen trailed after him, alert for whoever had fired shells and arrows into the center of a busy roadway. Maybe coming here had been a mistake. Regardless, the journey wasn't off to a particularly auspicious beginning. His normally optimistic side rose to the fore in spite of everything.

Things can only get better from here.

Lars shot a sour look his way. "I helped myself to your thoughts. While I hope you are correct, we must exercise caution."

Garen clapped him on the back. "Concentrate on finding our lodgings. Whiskey and women should improve both our outlooks."

Lars laughed. "My cock is in as bad a shape as my stomach. Did you find any likely wenches aboard the ship? At least you were out and about."

"No women. Nary a one. Obviously not on the crew, but not among the passengers, either."

"And here I was imagining you enjoying the hell out of yourself in your berth."

Garen waved his right hand in the air. "Madame Five Fingers got a workout."

"Our kind do not fall prey to human diseases. I am certain Boston hosts ladies for hire. Perhaps we can locate some who still retain vestiges of youth and enthusiasm."

"Speak for yourself." Garen jutted his chin skyward. "I'm so unutterably charming, women fall into my lap."

"I have noticed," Lars murmured in a wry undertone. "In that case, lure two and send the one you do not want my way."

Garen scanned the streets and turned right when he saw a sign for their hotel. It was far more modest than he expected, but so long as the rooms were clean and hot water plentiful for baths, it should be fine.

"Not exactly London or Paris or Heidelberg," Lars murmured, mirroring Garen's thoughts.

He shrugged. "It was where my employer suggested I stay. If we don't like it, we can look for something more commodious tomorrow."

Lars gripped Garen's arm, forcing him to halt. "Two possibilities, old friend. Either this is the best Boston has to offer, or your employer does not hold you in much esteem."

Garen started to bluster a reply, but thought better of it and clamped his jaws shut. Lars was correct. They went back too far for him to argue the point. If this whole American Colonies idea turned out to be a bust, they could always book return passage to Europe.

LARS WOKE to light streaming through his room's single, dirt-crusted window, pleased to be almost completely recovered from his weeks at sea. The woman who'd pleasured him the previous night was long gone. She'd been competent—and not overly chatty. Two plusses in his book. He and Garen had shared a passable meal in the establishment's rather run down dining room. At least the spirits were decent. A bit young and raw for his taste, but he'd had worse.

He rolled to a sit and reached for yesterday's clothes, then changed his mind. He rummaged through a valise for something clean. Surely the hotel had a laundry service of some kind. He'd ask over breakfast. Because he had time, he sent his cat senses spiraling wide. He found humans, dogs, cats, and a variety of wild animals in the surrounding woods. There was even a hint of a different type of magic. When he homed in on it, he sensed a perversion of witch energy. Were shifters here as well?

Surely his kind had found their way across the Atlantic. Perhaps not large cat shifters, but wolves like Garen or bears or coyotes or birds. He muffled a snort. Like as not, other cat shifters had made his same error, only realizing they made pathetically poor sailors once it was too late.

"It did not kill me," he mumbled. "I can cross the ocean again." Bending to secure his bootlaces, he added, "Next time, I will be better prepared. I fear this New World will not be all Garen hopes."

As if his thoughts drew his friend, a muted knock sounded on his door. Lars stood, walked to it, and turned the deadbolt.

"Ready for tea and breakfast?" Garen asked, smiling broadly.

Of a height with Lars, Garen stood several inches over six feet with a well-muscled build. Blue eyes augured into Lars, twinkling with merriment.

Lars nodded. "Breakfast would be welcome. Do you suppose they have the ability to wash our clothing?"

"Yes. I already asked. Bring what you want cleaned." Garen winked. "I made friends with some of the servants."

Lars elbowed him. "One of the things I have always admired about you is your cheerful attitude."

"Girl flesh helps that along."

Before Lars could mine for details about Garen's night, heavy footsteps clumped toward them. Garen spun to face the open doorway. Power shimmered about him, but only another magic wielder would've sensed it.

A tall, raw-boned man with unevenly trimmed red hair came into view. Leather garments clung to his frame. He narrowed shrewd green eyes at them. "Which of you is Mister LeRochefort?"

"That would be me." Garen squared his shoulders. "And you are?"

"Tom Smith."

The lie pinged off Lars' shifter senses. For whatever reason, the man wanted to hide his true name, but why?

Garen frowned. Obviously, he'd picked up on the falsehood too. "My associate and I—" he gestured at Lars "—were about to have breakfast. Would you care to join us?"

The man drew his brows into a thick line that met over the bridge of his nose. "Not quite my plan for the day."

Lars readied power of his own. Whoever this Tom Smith was, it appeared he wasn't on their side. "What exactly did you have in mind?" Lars cut in.

The man's gaze whipped to Lars. "Who the fuck are you?" he grated out.

"Mister LeRochefort's associate. He already told you that." Lars moved a step closer. The man was large, but he could take him—if it came to that.

"You didn't give me a name."

"Well, the one you gave us is false." Garen spoke up. "The way I measure things, we're about even. You hunted me down for a reason. What is it?"

"Don't matter what my name is. My people hired you." He sneered, displaying a mouthful of missing and decaying teeth. "You're coming with me."

Garen shook his head. "I'm a free agent. I don't have to do anything I don't choose to." He motioned to Lars before turning his attention back to the stranger. "Tell you what, *Mister Smith*, my associate and I are going to eat something. I know I suggested you join us, but I've changed my mind."

Lars understood. He tucked his money pouch into his jacket and shouldered past the man, keeping him at bay while Garen locked his room and pocketed the skeleton key. Though he was ready for the man to start throwing punches or draw the knife that hung from a waist sheath, neither happened. Anger streamed from him in waves, though. Clearly, he'd been given orders and attacking them outright wasn't on the menu—at least not yet.

Rather than going into the dining room, Garen moved on out the front door. "Let's see if we can find another option."

"How about over there?" Lars pointed across the street at a saloon that was clearly open despite the early hour. They'd have some type of food.

Garen nodded and pushed through swinging doors into a dark space that smelled like moldy beer. Sawdust was scattered across the floor. They found a corner table, ordered bread and cheese, and waited to see if their visitor would show up—with reinforcements.

Lars began eating as soon as a young girl brought their food. If he was any judge, they'd be on the run soon. Who knew when they'd have the luxury of eating again. Unless they switched to their animal forms and hunted.

"There's other magic here," Garen spoke into his mind.

"Yes. I sensed it too, but our friend back in the hotel was merely human."

"I can't believe Mister Smith—or whatever the fuck his name is—works for the people I corresponded with. It doesn't feel right."

"For once we are in agreement." Lars drained a tankard of terrible tasting ale.

"Have you had enough?"

Lars glanced at the empty plate. *"Nothing more to eat. What do you have in mind?"*

Garen got to his feet, leaving a few coins on the table. *"There's a stable to the south. I can smell the horses."*

"These places always have back doors off the kitchens. I say we locate it. It may buy us a few minutes grace."

Garen favored him with a toothy grin and switched to spoken words. "Funny, but I was about to suggest the same thing." He headed in the opposite direction from the front door.

Lars followed him. They'd discovered quite by accident that their animals' ability to converse telepathically extended to their human forms. Blood cemented that particular bond. Regardless, it was a handy skill.

After a terse exchange with a very annoyed cook after they invaded his small, filthy cooking area, they followed an alley until they hit the rear of a large stable. "I'll procure two horses," Garen told him.

"What about a wagon for our things?"

Garen twisted to face him. "Any idea how we can return to the hotel without tipping our hand?"

"I am certain someone is watching for us. If we do not emerge from the saloon soon, they will look more closely. If I were them, I would have a man posted near the stable." He pressed his lips into a thin line. "Our resources are far from infinite. We will need what we brought if we are to survive here."

"We'll play it your way." Garen nodded tersely. "I'd rather stand and fight than hide."

"This is Boston, not the western frontier. I do not believe anyone will take us on in broad daylight. Not until we have cleared this town's boundaries. Then all bets are off."

"Let's hope you're right."

Lars hoped he was too. While Garen dickered for horses and a wagon with a canvas cover to protect their things, he considered their next move. It made sense to remain near Boston. They needed work, and Boston was the primary staging area for the rebellion he suspected was imminent. It was only a matter of time before the Colonies waged out and out war to rid themselves of the yoke of British sovereignty.

The question of the hour was which side to align themselves with. Garen had already picked the Colonies. It made sense, but Lars wasn't totally convinced—yet. He rounded the corner of the stables and met Garen in front. He was still talking with the stableman, so Lars took a good, hard look at the two horses.

Both appeared sturdy, and neither flinched when he approached. Many horses were sensitive to shifters. Fortunately, not this pair. The wagon had seen better days, but the beaten metal around the wooden wheels wasn't too pitted.

Garen jumped onto the box and clucked to the horses. Lars swung up next to him as they began to move slowly up the street toward Newport House. It only took half an hour to transfer their belongings. Lars worked on that, while Garen settled up with the innkeeper.

Lars felt edgy, ready for anything, but they were the only ones moving about the hotel. He joined Garen in time to hear the innkeeper ask, "Where might you two gentlemen be heading next?"

"Not certain," Garen mumbled and turned away.

"Surely you know which direction," the innkeeper inserted smoothly. "North? South?"

"We'll figure it out as we go," Garen called over a shoulder. He glanced at Lars once they were outside. "Do we have everything?"

Lars nodded. "It is one of the benefits of not being here long enough to unpack. How is our gold coin holding out?" He climbed onto the high box, waiting for Garen to join him.

"The horses and wagon set us back a bit." Garen checked the ropes securing the canvas before springing onto the wagon's seat. He chirruped to the horses, and they headed out of town at a trot. "Innkeeper seemed a little too interested in our destination."

"I thought the same. I have been considering what it means."

"Did you come up with anything?" Garen scowled.

"*Ja,* but you will not like it."

"Try me."

"We are very good at what we do, you and me," Lars began. "Much of the behind the scenes maneuvering around the American Colonies is taking place in England. Someone likely wanted to get you out of the way. Make certain you were not available to spy for the other side."

Garen laughed uncomfortably. "I'm not that competent for them to go to all this trouble."

"All what trouble?" Lars furled his brows. "We paid for our own passage. Likely once we were here, without our usual complement of comrades, whoever has it in for you figured they could pick you off easily." He paused. "What they did not bargain for was that you would bring me along."

"I'm having trouble seeing either of us as that important."

Lars shrugged. "Fine. You come up with an explanation then."

"I don't have one, but I do have an idea for what comes next."

"Oddly enough, so do I." Lars gestured. "You first."

"There's opportunity here, but I'm sick of answering to anyone."

Lars stifled a grin. Maybe, just maybe, Garen was going to suggest exactly what he'd been thinking. "Go on."

"I say we form our own troupe of spies. We certainly have enough experience. I'd prefer to limit our new enterprise to shifters, though."

Lars sucked in a startled breath. He hadn't considered that aspect, but it made sense. From many angles. Shifters were intensely loyal to one another, stronger than humans, healed far more quickly, and lived hundreds of years. Sometimes over a thousand.

"You're not saying anything," Garen observed.

"Because I had not considered the shifter angle."

"Does that mean you came to the same conclusion about creating our own organization?"

"It does, but I see one small problem."

"What's that?" Garen asked.

"I am far from certain there are any shifters on this side of the Atlantic—beyond you and me, that is."

"Easy enough." Garen glanced his way. "We import them from the Old Country."

"*Ja*, and we will not tell the cats about how difficult ocean crossings are." Lars smiled broadly just before his nostrils flared. Something didn't smell right.

He opened his mouth to tell Garen to move the team off the road when Garen said, "I sense it too. Shit! That didn't take long."

"Why would it?" Lars asked pragmatically. "The longer head start we had, the harder it would have been to find us." He leapt from the box before the wagon quit rolling. "Move the fight away from the horses," he shouted.

"I'll be there as soon as I tie them up," Garen shouted back. "No point in them running all the way back to the stable."

"I'm more worried about them getting shot," Lars countered and took off at a dead run, shifting as he went.

GAREN SHIFTED, heedless of his clothes ripping. He could collect his boots afterward. The rest didn't matter. Fighting in his animal form was logical. The wolf was stronger and faster. Bullets were an impediment, but muskets were notoriously difficult to aim, and his wolf could dodge most rifle fire.

Lars' mountain cat was a sleek, silvery color with charcoal eyes. Garen ran hard toward where he stood in an aspen thicket atop a small rise. It was a good location because it afforded them a three-hundred-sixty-degree view and some cover.

He scented the air, grateful for his wolf's augmented sensitivity. That odd magic tang he'd noted earlier was back in spades. Good he'd chosen his shifted form. Magic against magic made sense. He drew alongside Lars and stared at four black-robed men running toward them. Still a quarter mile away, they were closing fast.

"Are they priests?" Garen asked.

"Not from any religion I know about. They are not carting rifles, so they must feel confident their magic will prevail." He nudged Garen with his snout. *"This employer of yours. Did you tell them you were a shifter?"*

"Of course not." Garen smothered irritation. *"Give me credit for a little sense."* He tossed his power in a wide net and blew out a surprised breath. *"Son of a bitch. They're witches."*

"Same scent I caught back at the hotel. It took me a while to recognize it because it's odd. More smoke and cedar than normal."

"Agreed, but that's what they are. Maybe there're different varieties here. We burned most of the ones in Europe."

"They hung them here, but that is not important. At least so far, they believe they are tracking our wagon. While we have the element of surprise on our side, you circle from the right. I will take the left."

"Two each?"

"Ja. Zwei. Leave at least one alive so we can interrogate him."

"Let's wait to see what they have in mind." Garen paused. *"I'm not averse to killing them, but let's wait until they declare war on us."*

"They already have. While we are waiting for them to proclaim themselves, we should get into position."

Garen melted from the clearing, sticking to tree cover and scattering power to hide himself. His wolf loved the prospect of a good fight even more than he did in his human form, but he recognized the wisdom of not killing humans for sport.

The man in the lead halted precipitously and kicked his head back, snuffling. He raised both hands, and the other three halted next to him, fanned out in a row. Garen felt the zing of power and figured they were communicating with one another. He didn't know much about witchcraft. Magic wielders were notoriously insular, unwilling to join forces outside their particular brand of power.

He scanned the men, assessing his two targets. One was tall and thin, the other more muscular. All had beards and shaved heads. The air took on an electric quality, almost as if it danced to the witches' orders. Two turned toward Garen, the other two toward where Lars hid in dense undergrowth. Power flowed from their raised hands. It held compulsion that made Garen's skin crawl. Bright, sharp heat broke over him, and he understood he had to move now, while he still could. If he hesitated, the witches' magic would snare him.

Shaking off the urge to surrender to the witches—run right into their trap—he moved closer, preparing to spring. The first two men would be easy. The others much harder since they'd scarcely sit back while their companions were murdered.

A streak of silver landed atop one of the men. Lars and the witch crashed to the ground in a swirl of power, grunts, and shouts. Garen switched objectives fast. One of the men drew a lethal looking knife. Before he could shove it into Lars, Garen arced through the air and landed on him, driving him to his knees.

He snarled and snapped, sinking his teeth into the man's neck. Blood, hot and coppery, jetted from torn vessels, drenching his pelt with gore. Something landed on his back, and liquid fire raced up one side.

Goddammit. Obviously his victim wasn't the only one with a knife.

Lars punched into his human body and leapt on the man who'd stabbed Garen. Wrenching the knife from his hand, he plunged it into his chest, driving it deep.

The fourth man turned and ran for all he was worth. Garen gave chase, catching him easily. He threw himself over the man's back, paws on his shoulders, and held him on the ground with the weight of his body. The man writhed and cursed, but Garen held fast. It would've been easy to kill him, but they needed information and the other three were well past speech.

Lars raced to his side. "I have this one."

Garen wasn't so certain. He held his position until Lars hooked the man's arms behind his back and bound them with a leather thong. He straddled the man's ass and held a blade to the side of his throat.

Satisfied their prey wouldn't escape, Garen drew on his magic and shifted, still breathing hard. "Who sent you?" he rasped. His side burned, and he threaded healing power toward where the knife had sliced through skin and muscles.

The man remained silent.

"If you tell us, we may allow you to leave alive," Lars said.

Garen heard coercion beneath his words.

The other man laughed. "Not very fucking likely, mate."

A snort blew past Lars' lips. "Your courage is misplaced." Lars pressured the knife against the man's neck until a thin line of crimson formed, weeping droplets of blood. Magic hovered around him, urging the man beneath to give up his secrets.

"Your power's wasted on me," the man gritted. "Save your time and kill me. I'll never talk."

"Braver men than you have eaten those words." Lars switched to mind speech and added, *"Take your wolf form and start with his feet."* He'd meant the words for Garen, but a low whine of fear escaped his victim, and he bucked against Lars' hold.

Garen pulled the man's boots off before reaching for his wolf. *"What do you think?"* he asked Lars. *"One toe at a time? Or should I just bite the foot off at the ankle?"*

The man writhed beneath Lars. Fear rose from him in choking waves that smelled like carrion.

"It appears he can hear us," Lars observed.

"I noticed the same thing."

As soon as his wolf solidified, Garen struck fast, closing his powerful jaws over the man's big toe. Bone snapped, and more blood splattered him. He spat the digit into the dirt to the accompaniment of bellows of pain. Ever methodical, he went for the next toe in line. It joined its brother in the dirt.

The man's bellows shifted to howls. The acrid stench of urine burned Garen's sensitive nose, and he understood the man's bladder had released. In spite of everything, he remained stubbornly silent beyond his cries of pain.

"Keep going," Lars urged. *"We do not have all day."*

Garen bent his head. Before he could snap off a third toe, the man screamed. "Stop. No more. I'll tell you what you want. Just stop."

Garen sent his shifter magic auguring into the man, seeking truth. He found it and pushed back into his human body. "I asked you once," he snarled. "Who sent you?"

"I work for the British Colonial government." The man's voice was muffled since Lars still held him face down in the dirt.

"Let him up," Garen said.

Lars shrugged. "Why not? It is not as if he can run from us." He swung off the man's body and stood by Garen's side.

The man dragged himself to a sit and covered his mutilated foot with a hand. A jolt of magic turned the air iridescent.

"No matter how much power you summon, you'll never get those toes back," Garen muttered.

The man trained dark eyes on him. "All I want is to stop the bleeding. I'll never walk right again."

"I wouldn't complain. You're still alive." Garen jerked his chin downward. "Why do your masters want me dead?"

The man's eyes turned to slits. "I have no master beyond Gaia, goddess of the earth. Witches retain independence."

"Fine. Fine." Lars clamped his jaw into a terse line. "Why were you after us?"

"Two reasons. You're shifters, and you were hired by the rebels. We can't allow them to add magic to their bag of tricks."

Garen frowned. "We called on our animal forms today, but how else would you have known something like that?"

Despite a face glazed with pain, the man managed a supercilious half smile. "It's why the Brits use witches. We sense other magic wielders."

"Not in Europe, you do not," Lars put in.

"Right." The man nodded once, sharply. "We're stronger here."

"How?" Lars pressed.

"Native magic strengthened ours. The shamans like us. They shared their power."

"Is that how you intercepted our mind speech?" Garen asked.

"Yes." The man opened his mouth but shut it before anything else came out.

"Fascinating," Lars muttered. "How many others will come after us?"

The question seemed to stymie the man. He hesitated and finally said, "Not certain. The group I worked with is all dead but me. Mostly they don't tell us anything beyond our assignments."

Garen understood. It was the same way he ran operations. "Did you tell those you report to that we're shifters?"

The man shook his head. "Didn't get the chance. We weren't certain until we got close enough to scent your power."

With a muffled grunt of pain, the man pushed to his feet. "I don't know anything else." Truth pinged off his words.

"One last question," Lars said.

"Yeah?" the man eyed him warily and rolled his weight back from the balls of his feet.

"Are there others like us here?"

For a moment the man looked confused. "Other shifters?" At Lars' nod, he went on. "Not many, but they're here. It's part of Native magic. They become one with an animal's spirit and take on its form."

Garen digested the information while the man walked slowly toward the dirt track. A cacophony of howls told him coyotes had already found the three corpses and were feasting merrily. The man had been cooperative, but they couldn't let him live. Garen caught Lars' eye. They'd worked together long enough, words weren't necessary.

In a flurry of glistening light, Lars' mountain cat streaked toward the man. A single paw swipe knocked him to the ground before Lars severed the vessels in his neck. It was a clean death. As close to painless as possible. Another flash of light, and Lars was human again, trotting toward Garen's side.

He grimaced, shaking blood off himself. "The witch dealt fairly with us, but we had no choice. He would have told his masters—the ones he claimed not to have—what we are."

"No, we didn't have a choice," Garen agreed. "Not so sure about *dealing fairly*. He only ponied up the truth because we cornered him."

Lars laughed wryly. "When you get down to brass tacks, it is sometimes the only reason anyone lets go of the truth."

Since their ripped clothing wasn't worth collecting, Garen

crooked two fingers at Lars, and they headed for where they'd left the wagon and team.

"You are quiet," Lars observed. "Does your side hurt?"

"You too," Garen countered. "Where we come from, we're born shifters. It appears there's more than one route to joining with an animal bondmate."

"Your injury," Lars pressed.

"I'll live. I'm not bleeding anymore. Another few hours, and my wound should be healed."

The horses whickered nervously, put off by the stench of blood, and Garen cursed softly. He should've thought to wash it off. The countryside hosted myriad small creeks. His wolf would've licked himself off, but he wasn't inclined to do the same in his human form.

He glanced at Lars. "We need water, so we don't totally spook the horses."

Lars detoured to a stream and stepped into it, squatting to sluice muddy water over himself. Garen joined him. "You missed a spot."

Lars made a huffing noise, not unlike his cat. "I probably missed many spots, but it will have to do. Even though we left no witnesses, we should be gone from here before much longer."

A few more handfuls of water later, Garen slipped and slid over moss-covered rocks. By the time he reached the wagon, Lars was partially dressed. He handed a muddy towel to Garen.

"Thanks." He dried off and dug clothes out of one of his valises, dragging trousers over his legs and a shirt over his head. "We can find our boots between here and the dead witches."

"Mine are in the wagon." Lars cast a knowing look his way. "I removed them before I left."

"Well aren't you Mister Think Ahead," Garen sniped.

"Finish dressing. I will retrieve your boots." Lars took off at a lope. He was back so quickly, Garen hadn't finished untying the team.

~

ONCE THEY WERE UNDERWAY, Garen said, "At least this clarifies it was truly the revolutionaries who hired me. I'd begun to wonder. The British have resorted to counter-espionage more than once."

"It also appears they were not aware they hired one with power."

Garen grinned. "Yeah, leave it to the Brits to ferret that out."

Lars snapped the reins lightly, and the horses picked up their pace. "They are world-renowned spy-masters. Beyond that, today's encounter sheds light on something for me."

"What might that be?"

"I feared you might have chosen the wrong side in the battle that is sure to sweep through the Colonies soon."

Garen laughed. "Same thing occurred to me—until we figured out the witches worked for the Brits. I'd rather die than work for those bastards. Not keen on working for the revolutionaries either, though. They did a deucedly poor job of guarding information regarding my arrival." He straightened his shoulders. "Didn't we decide we weren't going to work for anyone but ourselves?"

"We did, but we have yet to flesh out the finer points. Where to?"

"Back to Boston, but not right away."

"Say more, old friend."

"Boston is fairly large. We were only easy to find since they knew what ship we'd be on, and I was dumb enough to stay where they told me to." Garen shook his head hard. "What the hell was I thinking?"

Lars tossed one hand in a typically Teutonic gesture. "Had I not been so racked with seasickness, I might have—"

Garen waved him to silence. "It doesn't matter. I believe we can enter Boston quietly enough, no one will bother us. After a few days elapse, that is."

"How will we spend that time?" Lars furled his blond brows.

"Thinking through our new business. Fleshing out the details. How else?"

Nodding thoughtfully, Lars said, "We need a name."

"Aren't most spy operations incognito?"

"We are breaking with tradition. Developing a solid framework. I say we need a name."

Garen mulled it over as the horses' hooves clopped through packed dirt and mud. Birds cawed overhead, and a light rain began to fall.

"Since we are not returning to Boston immediately, we should shelter beneath some trees. Soon it will rain harder, and I would welcome a meal. Killing is hungry work."

Clucking to the horses, Garen urged them away from the track and into the woods bordering both sides of it. "How about Rubicon?" he asked.

"Huh?" Lars turned his gray gaze on Garen as if he'd lost his mind. "You mean the river in Northern Italy?"

"The same."

"What about it? We are far from there."

"We'll name our venture Rubicon."

A slow smile warmed Lars' eyes until they smoldered like coals. "Perfect. Ancient Roman law forbade anyone crossing the Rubicon with a standing army and entering Italy. Julius Caesar thumbed his nose at the rule and marched his troops across—"

"—Against all hope and expectation, the Roman legions offered him fealty," Garen finished the tale.

"Nothing wrong with your history."

"Maybe the name will work as well for us as it did for him." Garen drew the horses to a halt and swung down, sheltering under a tree to get out of the worst of the rain.

Lars joined him. "A sound thing to hope for."

"Maybe so." Garen smiled crookedly. "What about the Native shamans who befriended the witches? Do we want to explore their power too—if they'll accept us?"

"The prudent path is to leave them alone," Lars said thoughtfully.

"Even though they also bond to animals, there will likely be no love lost between our two varieties of shifter magic."

Garen nodded slowly. "You're probably right. We should start with our own kind—and stick with them."

"Agreed. There is money in the spy game. Opportunity. It will take time for us to send for our associates in Europe, but Rubicon will be stronger if we build it slowly."

"I have another idea," Garen cut in. "Once we're more or less established here, I can run things on this side of the Atlantic—"

"And I can operate Rubicon in Europe. I like it." Lars made a sour face. "So long as I survive the next ocean crossing."

"I'll come along to make certain you do. And to help establish our presence in Europe." Garen paused, thinking. "Neither of us will be leaving for a few months. Winter's nearly here."

"True enough, and if my shifter senses see true, the Colonies will be embroiled in a full-scale rebellion sooner rather than later. We can make ourselves useful—to the revolutionaries. If we are astute, we will earn enough to give ourselves a foundation for future years." Lars moved deeper beneath a stout evergreen. "Heidelberg would make a most excellent European location for Rubicon. Centrally located. Easy to slip into other countries and back again."

"And you just happen to have a manor house there." Before Lars could offer more arguments, Garen added. "It's a solid choice. Much better than Paris or London or Berlin."

"I am moving off the topic, but I am hungry. We do not have any food, so—"

"Feel like a hunt?"

"Want to get the taste of toes out of your mouth, do you?"

Garen laughed and removed his clothes. Even if they only scared up field mice, they were a decent meal, so long as he caught several of them. "We can hammer out the fine points once our bellies are full."

"Good enough for me." Lars stuffed his folded clothing beneath the wagon's canvas covering.

"Ready?" At Lars' nod, Garen summoned power and let his wolf form take over. America was shaping up to be a grand adventure. He and Lars would create the toughest, most ingenuous spy company the world had ever known. It would be a success because they'd only train and hire shifters. Before things were done, they'd both be rich men. He knew it down to his bones.

BOOK DESCRIPTION: LARS

Roll the clock forward a couple of centuries. Weapons have changed. Technology entered the scene, but espionage never fell out of fashion. Neither did the people who put their lives on the line keeping evil at bay.

Tamara MacBride has a much bigger problem than hiding her shifter side from the world. By the skin of her teeth, and with a smattering of Irish luck, she manages to kill her sister's murderer. Escaping from the scene of the crime is much harder than she anticipated. Just when she thinks she might be safe, her cab driver shrieks and slumps over the wheel.

An unknown assailant terminates Lars Kinsvogel's target. Pleased by the outcome—after all dead is dead—he exchanges the glitz of Monte Carlo for a nearby airport, intent on collecting the private plane he left there. He's no sooner arrived when a cab jumps the curb, and he races over to investigate. There's not much he can do for the cabbie, but his passenger is still very much alive.

Trying to hustle Tamara out of the cab is tough. She's frozen by fear, but when Lars lays out the rest of his plan to move her out of danger's path, her temper flares. He can't leave her alone in Monte Carlo. Can he convince her to trust him in time to save her life?

CHAPTER 1

*L*ars Kinsvogel sucked in an annoyed breath. Anxiety and greed thickened the air in Monte Carlo's Place de Casino, and he stifled a choking sound. Damn his hypersensitive shifter senses. If it weren't for them, the desperation hovering around him wouldn't be quite so palpable. Casinos were always like this, though, a haven for the rash and reckless. What had likely begun as a harmless pastime turned into hardcore addiction for an unfortunate few, forcing them to return again and again despite diminishing returns.

Hope springs eternal. All the poor sods need is one more spin of the wheel, another hand of cards... Lars glanced up, right into the croupier's beady gaze.

"Would monsieur like to place a bet?" The croupier grinned with all the warmth of a hammerhead shark, displaying a mouthful of bad teeth. What was it with the French and their aversion to dentistry? Lars shook his head and made shooing motions with one hand. He'd have to either join the baccarat game soon or move on, but he could get away with loitering for a few more minutes without drawing undue attention to himself.

His target, a powerfully built man with features revealing

Chinese ancestry, had an arm slung around a striking brunette. Maybe she was one of the hookers who worked the casino circuit, or maybe she was a steady thing for the man.

Lars considered it and decided she could be both. Around five feet eight, she had a lush, curvy body, dark hair cut into a stylish bob that fell a few inches past her shoulders, and memorable eyes the color of a restless ocean. A short, black sheath hugged her like a second skin. Open nearly to her waist, it displayed half her full breasts. Even though Lars' appraisal was surreptitious, he forced his gaze elsewhere. The woman was sex incarnate, and he didn't need anything diverting him from his objective.

Jaret Chen pressed chips into his companion's hand and urged her to pick a number. He gave one of her breasts a familiar squeeze, which earned him a smile, perfectly rouged lips stretching over impossibly straight teeth—and a slight shake of her head. Color stained her tanned skin. Lars realized he was looking at the woman again, wondering how her breasts would feel beneath his fingers. She seemed uncomfortable with Jaret's frank exploration of her body, so she probably wasn't a pro. For some unexplained reason, Lars felt relieved. The woman was too elegant to earn her living lying on her back.

He snorted to himself and studied the flashing display above the baccarat table. Maybe the woman wasn't French. That might explain her perfect teeth—and her discomfort with having her body mauled in public. At least she held Jaret's attention. So far the drug dealer hadn't spared him so much as a sidelong glance. Lars had never met the man, but knew a great deal about him from an extensive dossier provided by Rubicon International. Deeply involved in the heroin trade from the Middle East, across the Mediterranean, and into Europe, Jaret was one of the principals in a large operation—and Lars' current target.

He sized the man up. Maybe six feet, he had a barrel chest. Strongly muscled arms strained against the fabric of his cream-colored, silk dress shirt. His art deco tie had been loosened. Dark eyes, pronounced cheekbones, and straight dark hair cut short blended with his business attire. For all intents and purposes, he was indistinguishable from the phalanx of wealthy—and wannabe wealthy—men circulating through the casino. Lars glanced at his own cream-colored silk shirt and black linen pants. With the exception that his tie was still firmly knotted, he and Jaret were dressed as twins.

Guess neither of us wanted to stick out in anyone's memory.

Lars glanced at his Rolex. Close to midnight and time to move on. He'd seen enough. Now it was a matter of figuring out where and when to strike. These things always went more smoothly when he was close to invisible. He melted into the crowd and made his way outside. The casino fronted the French Riviera, and Lars stood looking out at the Mediterranean for long moments. The water was quiet tonight, waves barely slapping the white sand beach. His cell phone, set on silent, vibrated against his hip, and he tugged it from a pocket to look at the display.

Private. *Damn!* Could be anyone.

Lars punched the answer icon, held the phone to his ear, and waited. No need to say anything until he knew who was on the other end.

"Are you somewhere you can talk?"

Lars inhaled sharply as Garen LeRochefort's voice came through the phone's speaker.

Another shifter, Garen had founded Rubicon International with Lars hundreds of years before. The mechanics of the spy game had changed drastically between the late seventeen hundreds and modern times, but the basics—kill or be killed—hadn't altered much. Everyone who worked for Rubicon International was some type of shifter. Lars' animal form was a mountain lion, Garen's a wolf.

Lars loped farther down the beach until he cleared several couples engaged in deep, hungry kisses before responding. "What has happened?" Something must have, or Garen wouldn't have risked contact.

"You need to leave."

"But I have not—"

"Doesn't matter," Garen cut in. "I'll explain when you're back in the office on a fully encrypted line."

Lars thought about his twin engine Piper Seneca waiting at the Nice airport, twenty-four kilometers from Monte Carlo. It gave him freedom to come and go, and was much cheaper to operate than the business class jets he also owned. "Maybe I could still—"

"No!" The one word thundered so loud, Lars moved the phone away from his ear. "Don't even go back to your room." Garen hesitated. "Old friend. Trust me on this." The line went dead.

Lars stared at the iPhone's display and dropped the device back into his pocket. He'd been compromised. He wasn't certain quite how, and a part of him was curious as hell. He kept walking, swinging in a wide circle to head back toward the Hotel de Paris. Garen had said not to return to his room, but if he was careful, maybe he could learn something critical that would help their side.

"*Ja,* forewarned is forearmed," he muttered.

Keycard in hand, he let himself into a side door of the rambling old structure, got his bearings, and started cautiously up a stairwell. His suite was on the second floor, at the very end of the wing facing the Mediterranean. He'd always loved the old hotel with its thick, patterned carpets and antique lighting and furnishings. Staying next to the walls, he used a bit of shifter magic to cast a *don't look here* spell. It wouldn't keep someone determined from seeing him, but it didn't require much magic, either.

He entered the second floor a few doors from his own and scanned the empty hallway, his senses on high alert. Midnight was early in Monte Carlo, a city where people frequently stayed up through dawn and slept the day away, so he fully expected to see other guests, but the hall was mercifully empty. He padded silently toward his door and examined it, wishing he'd set a trap. He inhaled, trying to sort scents, but there were too many to make sense of. He could leave, just walk away like Garen had almost ordered him to, but Lars had never been a coward, and he was more intrigued than frightened. He'd spent years worming his way out of dicey situations. This was just one more, and he was damned if he'd walk away from his things. Not unless he had to.

He took a deep breath, tugged his guaranteed-not-to-set-off-metal-detectors .32 caliber revolver from its ankle holster, and shoved the key card into the slot in the door. A tiny electric motor hummed before the deadbolt snicked out of the way. He turned the latch, kicked the door open, and pivoted from side to side, scanning the sitting room of his suite, gun at the ready. Lars waited in the doorway, barely breathing, and then he heard a muted click, followed by an unmistakable whirr, and knew.

A bomb.

He cursed in German, not knowing if he was more annoyed with the turn of events or with himself for not taking Garen's advice and getting the hell out of there.

TAMARA MACBRIDE PUSHED the betting chips back into Jaret's hand. "Sure and I'm not feeling like wagering just now," she murmured. "Why don't you do it for me?"

He shot her an odd look. "But you like to gamble."

You only think I do.

"Something we had for supper didn't quite settle. Would you mind if I sat somewhere?" She swayed a bit on her feet to make her statement more realistic and sent a weak smile his way. In truth, she was a bit nauseated. Between sweat and greed, the air in the casino stank of humanity's darker side. Expensive colognes added a queer edge, their rich scents intensifying as their owners' anxiety rose. If she hadn't been a shifter, she might not have noticed, at least not as much. So far, she'd done a decent job hiding what she was from Jaret. She aimed to keep things that way.

He ran a thick index finger down the bare skin between her breasts. "We could return to our rooms."

She crinkled her face in what she hoped looked like an apology and did her best to ooze regret. "Better wait until my tummy settles." He was arrogant enough, he had no idea how repulsive she found him. Thank all the bloody saints, she'd managed to keep any sexual activities between them tamped down to nothing because of his heroin habit. According to a bit of Internet research, she supposed he could probably get hard, but the drug suppressed orgasms. At least so far, he'd been much more interested in his next shot of dope and drifting into an opiate-induced dreamy void than in bothering her for sex.

Jaret returned his attention to the baccarat table. "I'll just be over there." She pointed to a row of padded Louis Fourteenth chairs with bowed legs. Jaret nodded absently. His pupils were very small, so he was still fully under the influence of his last shot. That meant she had at least a couple of hours before he'd need to leave the casino.

Tamara tottered to a chair on ridiculously high heels. They made her feet ache, but Jaret liked it when she dressed like a fancy woman and pleasing him was high on her list. She settled onto the plush seat and slipped her shoes off. A waiter stopped and arched an inquiring brow. Nodding pleasantly at him, she ordered club soda. Rubbing the bridge of her nose between two fingers, she made a grab for her courage. So far, her plan had gone off without a hitch. The only thing left was to finish things off.

The waiter handed her drink over, along with a bowl of salted nuts, and she set both on a nearby chair. The ebb and flow of noise in the crowded room eddied around her. A quick glance at Jaret reassured her that he was still deeply engrossed in gambling—his second favorite addiction, right after heroin. He didn't care much for women, other than as window dressing and so the other men would see him as some sort of stud.

Tamara sipped her fizzy water and pursed her lips together. It was a long way from Dublin to Monte Carlo, and she wouldn't be here if it weren't for her sister. She bit her lower lip. Poor Moira. Dead at twenty-five. The coroner's report had listed a drug overdose as the official cause of death, but Moira hadn't been an addict. Her only crime was falling in love with Jaret Chen. Tamara had no idea how her sister actually died, but she knew in her bones that Jaret was responsible. Maybe someone had held her down while injecting enough of the crap to kill her.

She also had no idea how her sister could've been taken in by the Asian drug cartel lead-man, but Moira had always been drawn to powerful men. It was the only explanation.

She drained half her water and chewed a handful of cashews. Their entire family had been devastated by Moira's death, particularly her da. Tamara could still see his swollen, blotchy face at the funeral as he and three of her four brothers lowered the casket into the earth. The glass in her hand made an odd noise. She set it down before she broke it by accident. Moira had been a cat shifter, just like Tamara. Why the hell hadn't she claimed her animal form and killed the son of a bitch bent over the gaming table?

I'll never know.

She unclenched her jaw before her teeth cracked. She'd waited a few months so Jaret wouldn't be suspicious, and then searched him out. When he'd made a comment in passing that his last girlfriend had been Irish and had the same last name, she'd shrugged and blessed every goddess in the Celtic pantheon that Moira had the good sense not to tell Jaret anything about her family.

"MacBride's a common enough name in Scotland and Ireland," she'd informed him with a coy look, before asking, "What happened to her?"

"Who?" He'd looked the soul of innocence, the bastard.

"Sure and you know, your last girl pal. I'd hate to think she might come back to claim you." Tamara had held her breath then, torn between not wanting to hear whatever lie he came up with and being desperate for information.

He'd shrugged. "Hard to say quite what happened. Guess she dumped me." He'd made a sour face and muttered something disparaging about women under his breath.

That had been two months ago. In the intervening time, she'd inveigled her way into his life. Because she was attractive, pleasant, and never made any demands—easy enough since she couldn't bear the sight, or stench, of him—he'd allowed her into his inner circle.

She closed her teeth over her lower lip. The only thing she hadn't done was kill him. It would be easy enough. He slept like a dead thing because of his drug habit. She could do the deed and be out of their bedroom and on her way hours before anyone discovered his body. She'd never formally registered as a hotel guest. Jaret had his reasons for wanting her invisible. Apparently, he'd never guessed she might have her own.

So why haven't I finished this?

The answer bubbled up, and it sickened her. Nothing in her chosen profession as a freelance photojournalist had prepared her for wholesale slaughter. She was a coward, plain and simple. Killing in her mountain lion form was one thing. It felt...natural. Not that she'd ever killed anything except game to eat, even shifted. To take a life, in a cold-blooded, carefully thought out manner, repelled her. She'd dreamed of shoving her knife into Jaret's carotid, even circled him while he slept, blade in hand, but in the end she hadn't been able to force herself to strike.

Her hands ached because she'd balled them into fists. Once she uncrimped her fingers, blood welled where her nails had sliced into her palms.

Either I do this thing, or I need to leave.

An unpleasant thought surfaced. She was in so deep, he'd never just let her walk away. Maybe that had been Moira's undoing. Sick to death of playing third fiddle behind Jaret's addictions, maybe her proud sister had issued an ultimatum and ended up with enough heroin in her bloodstream to kill a moose.

The more she considered it, the more certain Tamara was she'd hit within spitting distance of the truth. She gazed at her lap and pulled the gaping front of her dress closer together. There wasn't any choice. Not really. He'd never let her go, so she had to latch onto enough moxie to finish him off.

"Another drink, mademoiselle?" The waiter was back. He stared at her half-exposed breasts, a lascivious grin not far from the surface.

She nodded. "Scotch. Single malt. Twenty years old, or more."

"Very good, mademoiselle. Anything to go with it?"

What could she order that wouldn't blow her upset stomach story? "Um, crackers, with some brie."

The waiter walked away. She stared after him. In a very distant way, he looked like the Teutonic god who'd been eyeing them from across the baccarat table earlier. The tall, blond man had been broad-shouldered and slim-hipped. His eyes were a cool, icy gray, and his facial bones damn near perfect, with a square jaw and pronounced cheekbones. He hadn't smiled, but she imagined his teeth would be very straight.

Why can't I have someone like that in my life?

Because I'm a shifter, goddammit. It's a big secret to keep.

Yeah, and to keep on keeping it made her weary. She'd given up on a normal life when the first change came on her shortly after she hit puberty. There were laws to ensure shifters didn't get out of hand that included killing them—or shipping them off to prison. It was prudent—and necessary—to hide what she was, rather than embrace it. Her parents, both shifters themselves, had hammered that point home until she was sick of hearing it.

The waiter had just stopped by with her drink and crackers with cheese when Jaret joined her. "Feeling better, I see." He pried the glass from her hand, swallowed half its contents, and raised his eyebrows. "Expensive."

"I can pay for it. I still have a little money."

He rolled his eyes. "No, no. Wouldn't dream of that. You're my woman, aren't you?" At her pleasant nod, he went on, "I take care of my women. Good care of them. Come on." He tugged her to her feet.

"Wait. My shoes." She bent and fished them from beneath her chair. Hanging onto him, she balanced first on one foot, then the other, while she slid her feet into the pumps. "Okay." She grinned broadly. "All ready."

"Do you want to bring the crackers along?"

"Sure. Why not?" She gripped the plate in one hand and curved the other around his arm. He finished her drink and steered them out of the casino toward the stairs that led to the Hotel de Paris.

Tonight, she told herself. *Before tonight's over, he'll be dead. Moira can rest in peace, and I'll be out of here.*

CHAPTER 2

Shock ran through Lars as he stood in the open doorway of his room. He clacked his jaw shut. This was a time for action, not contemplation. Someone had planted a bomb with a timer. Running on instinct, he yanked the door to his suite closed seconds before an explosion rocked the floor. He'd just jammed his gun out of sight when two hard-eyed men dressed in the casino's signature black shirts, blazoned with a red fleur-de-lis, raced into the hall. It figured the hotel would use the casino's security squad since the Place de Casino was right next door and managed by the same corporation.

"Monsieur. What happened?" The red haired guard loped to his side and stared at Lars with penetrating green eyes. Around fifty, he looked like he'd seen a lot. Lars knew better than to feed him a line of bullshit.

He ginned up a rattled expression. "Damn if I know. I had just opened the door to my suite when I realized I forgot my jacket in the casino. I pulled the door shut and turned to leave." He tossed his hands skyward. "The whole building shook." Lars jerked a thumb toward his room. "It sounded like something exploded in there. Is that even possible? My things…"

The other guard pulled out a small electronic device, traced the sides, top, and bottom of Lars' door, and muttered, "No fire. No poison gas."

"Maybe we should get the dog," the first guard spoke up.

"Dog?" Lars infused anger into his tone. "If your implication is I have something illegal in my room, I resent the hell out of it."

The second guard, a balding thirty-something with brown hair and mud-colored eyes shrugged. "Resent all you wish, monsieur. We see a lot here. The Mediterranean is a prime entry point for drugs from Africa and the Middle East."

Lars drew himself up. "May I go back into my room? See what has been damaged? I had a very expensive laptop, my clothes, the keys to my airplane."

"You own an airplane?" Guard number one exchanged glances with his cohort.

"Yes." Lars reached for his back pocket and found himself staring down the barrels of two .45 caliber semiautomatic pistols. He held his hands up. "Whoa, easy there, boys. I was just going to show you my passport and my ID. We are on the same side."

"We'll get them for you." Guard number two moved behind Lars and extracted his wallet and passport case. He flipped open the passport and handed Lars his wallet.

Lars pulled out a business card with Rubicon International's logo and handed it to the guard who wasn't examining his passport. A radio crackled. The red-haired guard spoke into it in French, telling the man on the other end everything was under control.

"Now that you know who I am, may we at least open the door to my suite to assess the damage?" Lars asked, taking his passport. He returned it to his back pocket, along with his wallet.

The first guard waved Lars' card under his nose. "What exactly do you do for this international security company?"

"Electronics. I program computers." Lars cocked his head to one side. "Though I hate to admit it, I am quite the desk jockey. Coming here was my first vacation in over a year, but it will be ruined if my laptop was trashed."

"You live in Heidelberg?" the second guard asked. "German national?"

Lars nodded. "Yes to both. You saw my passport."

The guards exchanged another glance. The redhead raised his eyebrows in a quizzical expression, and then used his own key card, obviously a master, to unlock the suite's door. "Stay back," he instructed Lars, "until we're certain there's no further danger."

It chafed, but Lars did as he'd been told and waited while the guards swept through his rooms. He heard a long, low whistle. That did it. He stepped inside. The balding guard hunkered next to a circular pile of shrapnel. Lars tightened his jaw, grinding his teeth together. Not a bomb. Not exactly. Compressed air, and enough shrapnel to kill him—if he'd been standing in just the right place. Even if he hadn't, flying debris would likely have wounded him. Lars had used similar devices. They were handy because damage was localized to a small area.

Once I was incapacitated, they would have let themselves in here and finished me off. Guess they did not factor hotel security into their equation.

Whoever was behind this probably fled as soon as the two security men showed up, but they had to have been close. Lars smiled sourly to himself and walked past one of the guards into the bedroom. Once there, he pulled his valise from the closet and started tossing clothes into it.

"You are leaving, monsieur?" The balding guard came up behind him.

Lars spun to face him. "*Ja.* Would you not do the same?"

"We know where to find him." The first guard pocketed Lars' card.

"Indeed." Lars glanced from one guard to the other. "Might one of you be so kind as to call for a private car to take me to the Nice airport?"

"Of course." The older guard spoke into his mouthpiece.

Lars grabbed his Dopp kit from off the bathroom ledge, dropped it into his valise, and zipped everything up. His next stop was for his laptop, which didn't look as if it had been touched. He stowed it and its charger into a hard-sided computer bag.

Stupid of them. They should have taken it the first time they were in here.

Not that it would've done them any good. The hard drive was programmed to self-destruct if anyone unauthorized tampered with his computer.

He slung his valise and computer bag over one shoulder and started out the door. The guards were taking samples of something and dropping them into sealed bags. One looked up. "Your car should be waiting. Will you be returning to the casino for your suit jacket?"

Lars drew his brows together. "Under the circumstances, no. I am a bit concerned about my plane. Airport security is impeccable, but still…" He let his words trail off.

The red-haired guard straightened. He met Lars' gaze. Lars stared back, his expression guileless. "If we find your jacket, we'll have hotel staff package it and ship it back to you."

Lars waved a dismissive hand. "You need not bother. I have dozens of suits. Furthermore—" he cocked his head to one side "—I have been gone from the casino for long enough, someone has likely stolen it by now."

The guard narrowed his eyes, and then a snort of laughter crept past his carefully constructed cop persona. "Maybe so." He shook his head. "Get going, monsieur. Those private cars are expensive, and you're on their meter from the moment they roll up to our door."

Lars didn't wait for a second invitation. He loped down the long hall to the stairwell closest to the front door. He'd just started down the risers when he heard footsteps and spun to see who'd followed him. Muscles so tense they felt like rocks, he yanked his gun out and stared upward.

Only the older guard. Lars dropped the gun into his pants pocket, but its outline was unmistakable against the linen fabric.

"Monsieur, we thought it prudent to accompany you." The guard looked meaningfully at Lars' pocket. "It appears you're more than you revealed."

"Mmph." Lars engaged the gun's safety and moved the revolver back to its ankle holster. He met the guard's green eyes head-on in a silent challenge to make something of it.

"If you were planning to stay, I'd make you leave that in the hotel safe. As it is…"

"Thanks." Lars trotted down the remaining stairs, with the guard flanking him. He started toward the front desk to settle his bill, but the guard hooked an arm through his and drew him off to one side.

"No need to visit the receptionist. We'll see the paperwork is closed out." He leaned close. "Can you think of a reason anyone would want you dead?"

Lars drew back as if he'd been whipped, congratulating himself for a stellar performance. "Dead?" He shuddered. "Absolutely not. Appreciate you taking on the front desk for me. My French is not quite up to par."

Without waiting for the guard to come up with another hard-to-answer question, Lars sprinted for the front door where a uniformed chauffeur scanned the crowd. "I believe you are hunting for me," he told the man. "Where is our car?"

"Right this way, monsieur." The chauffeur held his hands out for Lars' bags, but Lars shook his head.

"I am fine. They are not heavy."

"If you're certain, monsieur." The chauffeur hurried ahead and tugged open the limo's rear door.

Lars tossed his things inside and followed them. Though it was foolhardy, he deluded himself that the satisfying *thunk* of the door closing meant he was safe. He leaned against the plush upholstery of the limousine's rear seat and took a deep breath. The rich scents of leather and liquor filled his nostrils; there must be a bar behind one of the rosewood panels.

The chauffeur met his gaze in the rearview mirror. "I would offer you a drink, monsieur. You can help yourself."

Lars shook his head. "Sounds wonderful, but no thanks. I am flying."

The man glanced over a shoulder and winked broadly. "Rules are only rules if they catch you breaking them." Lars felt a chuckle bubble up. He let it go, pleased it lessened the tension in his gut.

The chauffeur merged the big car into heavy traffic. "What's so funny?"

Lars shrugged. "What you said was just so...French."

The chauffeur laughed too. "*Oui*, you Germans have a bit of a different world view. Rules, rules, rules." He tossed both hands in the air. The car swerved, and he made a grab for the steering wheel.

Lars shut his eyes for a moment, choreographing his next move. Should he fly back to Germany, or rent a business class jet, file an international flight plan, and head for New York? Perhaps the most discreet course would be to return to Germany and take one of his own jets, but that would take additional time. He'd just decided to call Garen and discuss his options when a loud boom rocked him. The limousine's rear window shattered, coating him with shards of glass.

Lars ducked below the level of the rear seat. "Drive," he shouted to the chauffeur. "I do not care how you do it, but get me to Nice and the airport I will pay you triple your normal rate."

"In a pig's eye. If you wish transport to a funeral, you'll have to drive there yourself." The driver sounded truly terrified, his voice high and screechy. The limo squealed to a stop, and he hurled headlong out his door, running for all he was worth the second his feet connected with pavement.

Cursing, Lars exited his door staying low, got behind the wheel, and took off. If luck was with him, the bad guys wouldn't try again because Monaco was crawling with cops. Part and parcel of the casinos, there were almost as many of them as there were gamblers. Maybe that would work in his favor.

TAMARA PARADED SLOWLY UP and down their hotel suite, trying to mimic a stripper and feeling nauseated. Damn the luck! Jaret had waited on more heroin, saying he wanted sex for the first time since she'd begun hanging around with him. Fortunately, he was doing himself. She hadn't offered, and he hadn't asked. He'd get close, and then he'd go soft and curse her.

"Look sluttier," he gasped. "I'm almost there."

She strutted, bumping and grinding her hips. When that didn't seem to do the trick, she tossed her head, hiding behind a sheaf of dark hair. Tamara racked her brain, trying to think of some exotic dancer moves, when he panted, "Frig yourself."

"Huh?" She spun and glanced at him, something she'd been trying to avoid. His face was blotchy and he had his cock in a death grip, but at least it was still hard.

"Sit in that chair—" he flung an arm outward "—and masturbate. I like to watch."

She swallowed her surprise. This was a new development, but then everything since they'd returned to their rooms was. Why couldn't he just shoot himself into oblivion and go to sleep?

He reached over and slapped her ass with his free hand. "Move it, bitch."

Tamara leapt away from him, settled onto the indicated chair, and closed a hand over each breast. She twirled her nipples into peaks before moving a hand between her legs. It was a long time since she'd come. She rubbed a finger over her clit, surprised to feel it swell beneath her ministrations. Maybe she wouldn't have to fake arousal. She shut her eyes, called up an image of the fine-looking blond from earlier that night, and rubbed herself. In no time, her hips bucked against her hand as an orgasm rocked through her.

"Yes," Jaret crowed from where he lay on the bed, jacking himself. "Do it again."

Tamara caught her breath. She'd been so lost in her fantasy of the blond stranger sinking his mythical long, hot cock inside her and fucking her senseless, she'd almost forgotten about Jaret.

"Sure and you're not wanting me to take care of you?" she asked, desperate to do something, anything, to get this over with faster, so she could get to the real business of the evening—killing him.

He shook his head. "No, I get hotter watching than anything else." His hand moved faster and faster on himself. "Frig yourself, babe. I want to watch you when I come."

She moved her fingers over her swollen clit again and shoved two fingers from her other hand inside her pussy. It felt damned good, too good. Her hands moved in a rhythm to match his as she thought of the blond again. She fingered her G-spot and shuddered against her hand about the same time he shrieked, and semen jetted from his red, swollen cock.

"We'll have to do that again, sweetheart," he crooned. "It takes time to get to know one another."

You mean time to get comfortable letting your perversions swim to the surface.

She bit back what she wanted to say and just smiled.

He swung his legs over the side of the bed and headed for the bathroom. Thank fucking God. He'd dose himself now and be asleep in no time. She crawled under the covers and waited, feigning sleep. Sure enough, the bedsprings creaked, he rolled over, and was snoring within a few minutes.

She kept an eye on the clock. When half an hour had passed, she eased herself from the bed.

Don't think. Just do.

She'd formulated this a hundred times in her head. A thousand. The suite's kitchen was fully stocked. She ignored its selection of knives and plucked her own from where she'd carefully hidden it in the bottom of her suitcase, gazing at the lethal expanse of steel.

She'd purchased the ten-inch blade right after they'd gotten to Monaco, during one of the rare occasions Jaret allowed her out of his sight. Tamara brought the blade to her lips, murmured a silent prayer, and tiptoed back into the bedroom.

This time, she didn't hesitate. She'd learned from her past attempts that if she took the time to do anything but strike, she'd lose her nerve. Jaret lay on his side, chin tipped, the vessels in his neck clearly outlined beneath his ruddy, Asian skin. The next few minutes would be hell. Would he attack her? It took time for people to die. Time for them to lose enough blood they were no longer a threat...

She sprang, plunged the knife deep, and swung it through jugular and carotid both. Jaret was slow, sluggish. He must've given himself a whopping dose of heroin, or else it had been stronger than he expected. Blood sprayed from his severed carotid, geysering several feet into the air. Shocked by the grisly scene, she hurtled off his body. He made a gurgling, whooshing sound and bounded off the bed right for her, driving her to the carpeted floor. She hoped the thud wouldn't bring security running.

Her heart pounded. Sweat slicked her sides. She stabbed again and again with the knife. He closed his hands around her throat, cutting off her air. She writhed beneath him until her eyesight grayed around the edges. Frantic and furious, her cat took over, forcing her way through. When her vision cleared, she was on top of him, mountain cat fangs buried in his gushing neck.

Knowledge flickered in the depths of his dark eyes. He opened his mouth, and blood burbled past his lips as he gasped. "You're her fucking sister. Abomination. Just like her."

She loosened her grip and jumped off his body. He wasn't quite dead yet, but it would be over very soon. Tamara reached for her human form, barely allowing herself to breathe. She had to get out of there, put distance between herself and Jaret's corpse. Bloody cat tracks peppered the beige carpet. She wasted precious moments working on them with hot water and a sponge before she gave it up for a lost cause.

Tamara doused her blood-soaked body in the shower, dried off, and dressed as fast as she could. She stuffed her few things into her suitcase—along with her knife—grateful Jaret had never registered her as a hotel guest. If she were any judge of things, he'd probably used some name other than his own at the front desk. Also a good thing, if it were true. She was fairly certain Chen was his real name, though most of his men used aliases.

Tamara dragged a dark coat over her jeans and black sweater, tied a scarf over her hair, and picked up the handle of her carry-on. Purse in her other hand, she crept to the door of the suite, opened it cautiously, and glanced out. Empty.

Thank Christ!

She walked down a back staircase and let herself out into the humid night. Tamara glanced around. Relief that she was still alone weakened her knees. Maybe one of the goddesses really was watching over her. She plucked the knife from her suitcase's outer zippered pocket, wiped it down carefully with her scarf, and dropped it into a hole in a thickly flowering hedge. So far, everything had gone better than she could have hoped.

Tamara padded silently away from the bulk of the hotel, rejoining the sidewalk about twenty yards past its ornate front doors. Disgust filled her when she understood she could've taken care of business weeks before and spared herself the degradation of her days—and nights—with her sister's murderer. At least his final words explained what happened to Moira. He'd discovered she was a shifter and killed her for it.

She waited until she was several blocks from the hotel before she hailed a cab and asked the driver to take her to the airport in Nice. Settling into the taxi's back seat, triumph surged, hot and vital.

I did it.

Yes, but I'm not in the clear yet. I still have to get out of here.

Even if she escaped, she'd met enough of Jaret's boys. They

weren't stupid. They'd put two and two together, figure out she'd killed him, and hunt her down. She squeezed her eyes shut as the enormity of what she'd done settled in her gut like a lead block.

One thing at a time. I can't fight tomorrow's battle until I get back home.

Her eyes widened. Maybe she shouldn't go home. Ireland would be the first place they'd look for her.

I'll figure it out when I get to the airport and see what my options are.

CHAPTER 3

*L*ars nursed the limo along in traffic that barely hit sixty-five kilometers an hour. The twenty-four kilometers between the hotel and airport had shrunk to less than eight, but his speedometer kept drifting left as one emergency vehicle after another sped past him. Every light, every siren, set his teeth on edge. He was certain the chauffeur had called someone by now and reported the shooting incident. Tightening his hands on the wheel, he hoped to hell the glass separating the passenger compartment from where he sat was bulletproof.

Another siren drew closer. Lights flared in his rear view mirror, and he loosed a string of German curses. It was obvious this cop car wanted him to pull over. Lars cut across two lanes of traffic, to the accompaniment of blaring horns, and exited onto the shoulder.

He got his wallet, passport, and international driver's license ready and rolled his window down.

"Sir?" A young, nervous looking man, one of France's Gendarmerie Nationale officers judging from his uniform, walked to the car's open window and shifted from foot to foot.

Lars stared at him, waiting, but the cop didn't say anything else.

"Tell me what you want," he growled and waved his passport, driver's license, and a business card at the policeman.

"You left the scene of a crime."

Accusation ran beneath the man's words. Tall and rangy, he had dark hair and pale eyes, lending him an anemic appearance. He scanned Lars' passport. When Lars decided he'd had it long enough, he snatched it back and handed the cop his business card. The cop started to reach in the window, intent on the passport in Lars' right hand.

"Not a good idea." Lars kept his voice mild and dropped his passport onto the passenger seat.

The cop drew back, looking cowed. "You left the scene of a crime," he repeated. "What do you have to say for yourself?"

"This vehicle was shot at. One of those wrong place, wrong time things, no doubt." Lars made an apologetic gesture with one hand. "I was unaware of any crime, certainly not one I committed. My driver left. I still needed to get to the airport, so I drove."

"Do you have airline tickets?" the cop asked. Lars shook his head. "What was the rush?" the cop blundered on. "If you didn't have tickets for a specific flight..."

Lars blew out an impatient breath. Maybe he could stonewall this joker who looked barely old enough to be out of secondary school. "I have my own airplane. My business called. They require my presence in the United States immediately. I—"

"Did you file a flight plan? If so, I'll need the number."

"No. I planned to do that when I got to the airport."

"What type of aircraft?"

"Excuse me?"

The cop narrowed his eyes. "You said you have a plane. What kind is it?"

"Piper Seneca."

The cop's frown deepened. "I wasn't aware they were capable of crossing an ocean."

What the fuck? Why am I having a conversation about aircraft capabilities in the middle of the night—with a cop?

"They can, but not without long range tanks and augmented avionics. I have jets in Heidelberg, but I was considering renting one in Nice to save time."

"Show me your pilot's license."

Thinking this was getting stranger by the minute, Lars reached for his computer case, and then remembered it was still in the rear seat.

"Keep your hands where I can see them, sir." The young man's voice held a slight tremor. Was this the first time he'd ever stopped anyone?

"Fine." Lars gritted his teeth. "My pilot certifications and log book are in my computer bag."

"Hand me the entire bag, sir."

"They're in the back." Lars located the button that retracted the glass between the passenger and driver compartments. Twisting in his seat, he retrieved both his valise and computer bag and chucked them on the seat next to him. He activated the electronics to close the glass panel, resisting an urge to shove the hard-sided computer case into the cop's solar plexus.

Behind the wheel again, he kept a hand on the computer bag but didn't push it through the window. Nor did he get his pilot's license out. Something was wrong. No cop worth anything would be taking all the time this one was. Unless he was waiting for reinforcements. "Show me your identification," he snarled.

"Excuse me, sir?" Something uncomfortable flitted behind the cop's unnaturally pale eyes.

"Your identification. All cops carry something beyond their badge."

The man swallowed. He was afraid. Lars smelled it. He'd never shut the engine off. Relying on intuition, he jammed his foot down on the accelerator. The powerful engine sprang to life, and the limo roared down the shoulder. He rolled up the window and merged into traffic that was moving faster than it had been.

"If I was wrong," he muttered, "I will be in a world of shit."

He pounded a fist on the steering wheel, gratified when a sign flashed past telling him the airport exit was in five kilometers. The man who'd stopped him hadn't been a cop. He couldn't have been. No. His job was to delay Lars long enough for others to catch up to him, probably the same bunch who'd shot out the limo's rear window. Taking his pilot's license would've been brilliant since he couldn't do anything without it. Now that he considered things, he was fortunate he'd snatched his passport back.

He activated a turn signal and took the airport exit. He'd ditch the limo in long term parking, and that would be that. Like everything else, finding a spot to leave the oversized vehicle took longer than he would have liked. Every minute that passed without a siren reinforced that the man who'd stopped him was an imposter. If he'd truly been part of the Gendarmerie Nationale, half a dozen cars would've converged on him by now.

Lars scanned the parking lot for threats before getting out of the car and glanced at the limo's keys, debating. The kindest thing would be to leave them, so he stowed them beneath a floor mat, grabbed his valise and computer bag, and sprinted for the shuttle stop a hundred yards away. People were milling around, which probably meant he'd be more-or-less safe. Lars shook his head. He didn't get it. Sure, he'd sidestepped the booby trap in his hotel suite, but it felt as if the dogs of Hell were breathing down his neck.

Why? It wasn't as if he'd taken out his target.

His phone vibrated. He fished it from his pocket, punched *Answer*, and held it to his ear. "Say something," Garen snapped, "so I know it's you."

Lars blew out a tense breath and stopped walking. He was still far enough from the crowd at the shuttle stop, they couldn't hear him. "It has been a rough couple of hours."

"No shit. Why the fuck didn't you do what I told you and get the hell out of Dodge?"

Lars shrugged, realized Garen couldn't see him, and said, "Since when do we take orders from each other?"

Garen snorted. "We don't, but you left a hell of a mess. Between the hotel room and the limousine—"

"Yes, well we can hope my airplane is still in one piece."

"We'll worry about the Piper later," Garen cut in. "I've paid additional hangar rent for them to keep it two more weeks. Go to Ermstatter International. I've arranged for a Gulfstream G280—and a copilot. You depart in—" Garen sucked in an audible breath "—just over an hour."

Lars chuckled to mask growing annoyance. "Did you also file my flight plan?"

"Now that you mention it—"

"Where am I landing?" Lars batted back irritation. He didn't need Garen to take care of him, goddammit.

"New York. You have an eight-hour layover in the private pilots' lounge at JFK, and then you'll come on into Seattle, and we can figure out what to do next."

"You know more than you are telling me."

It was Garen's turn to laugh, but it held a chilly edge. He sounded as out of sorts as Lars felt. "Of course."

"Is there anything else for now?"

"Miranda said to tell you she's looking forward to seeing you." He paused for a beat. "And congratulations on a job well done."

Lars smiled, his pique blown away like sand in propeller wash. "Tell Miranda the same back."

"I will." Garen disconnected.

Lars dropped the phone back into his pocket and thought about Miranda, Garen's mate. A stunning six foot tall brunette with sparkling blue eyes, she also worked for Rubicon International. As lethal as any man, she'd gotten her espionage training in the Green Berets. Miranda was a wolf shifter, just like Garen. Lars nodded to himself. He'd been interested in her, but she'd only had eyes for Garen. He wished them all the best, had stood as best man at their wedding...

He frowned. What had Garen said after mentioning Miranda? *Congratulations on a job well done?* What the hell? He hadn't done anything—other than rely on his wits to stay alive.

Lars bit his lower lip, thinking. He reached into his pocket and fingered the phone, half intent on calling Garen back, but curiosity wasn't a strong enough reason to add yet another risky phone conversation to the one they'd already had. Still feeling puzzled, he took his place in line with the other travelers. When the shuttle arrived moments later, he asked the driver to drop him at Ermstatter International.

"I can take you to the main terminal, sir. You'll need to catch a taxi from there. Ermstatter is half a mile away, but they share our runway system."

Lars nodded. Easy enough. He slung his traveling bags over his shoulders and hung on to a strap since all the seats were taken. It only took a few minutes before the shuttle rolled up in front of the main terminal building. Lars trotted down the steps and headed for a bank of taxis, intent on hiring one.

Brakes screeched. A cab rolled past the line of taxis, cut in front of them, and slammed into the curb. It teetered for a moment, jumped the curb, and came to a stop only a few feet from him. Its driver was slumped over the steering wheel.

Lars' instincts shouted a warning, and he moved in for a closer look. What the hell? Had the man had a heart attack?

Bullet holes riddled the doors and windshield.

Crap!

This place had turned as lethal as Afghanistan's mountains. Lars scanned the inside of the taxi. A woman hunched into a corner of the backseat. Was she hurt too? Or maybe dead? It was hard to tell how badly wounded the driver was.

As if they sensed imminent danger, people gave the taxi a wide berth. Probably for the best. It beat having a phalanx of nosy assholes breathing down his neck. Lars pulled the driver's door open and shut off the engine. He laid a hand over the driver's carotid and hunted for a pulse.

Dead, damn it. Poor bastard.

Lars cast his shifter senses spinning outward. Was the shooter still close? He'd pretty much have to be. Lars felt a familiar tightening in his gut and a prickling at the nape of his neck. Danger was indeed near, but moving away, not toward him. Amazed that airport security hadn't stormed them yet, he yanked open one of the back doors, intent on finding out if the woman had met the driver's fate—and heard a soft sob.

"Come on. It will be all right." He kept his voice, low, soothing. "Give me your hand, and let me get you out of here."

She raised her face from her trembling hands. Shock raced through him. It was her. The woman from the casino who'd been with Jaret Chen. What in the name of God was she doing here at the airport by herself, with a dead taxi driver? There were only a couple of answers that fit, and Lars didn't care for either of them. Suddenly, Garen's congratulations took on a whole new meaning.

Chen must be dead, and Lars might be looking at the woman who'd done it.

"Come on," he repeated. "We need to get you out of here." He closed a hand over her arm and dragged her from the taxi. She reached back inside and came up with a smallish suitcase and a shoulder bag.

"Who are you?" Her eyes were so wide with fear, only a small rim of blue showed around dilated pupils. Recognition apparently slammed home, and even the thin strip of blue disappeared. "I saw you," she blurted, looking panicked. "In the—"

He shook his head, wanting to shut her up. "No time for that, *fraulein.* I am not on their side. That will have to do for now."

She nodded mutely, suitcase clutched so tightly, her knuckles turned purple. She swayed on her feet. He hoped she wasn't about to sink into shock—or worse, faint. Lars wasn't sure quite what he'd do if that happened. He tucked a hand under her elbow and guided her a hundred feet to the first taxi in line, hoping like hell the driver wouldn't tell him to take a hike. Surely he'd seen what happened.

To forestall being turned down, Lars flashed a five hundred Euro note at the driver who palmed it and said cheerily, "Where to, sir?"

"Ermstatter." Lars took the woman's suitcase, handing it to her once she folded her leggy frame into the cab. He hustled in behind her and slammed the door. "There is another five hundred if you hurry," he told the driver.

"You got it, sir." The cabby's accent was pure Brooklynese. Lars wondered what a New York cabbie was doing in Nice. No wonder he'd turned a blind eye to the cab that jumped the curb—and its dead driver. He'd no doubt seen worse on the streets of New York. As they cruised past the disabled taxi, Lars noticed airport security had finally dispatched agents to look into the accident. Thank Christ he'd gotten Chen's girlfriend out of there in time.

Lars glanced sidelong at her. Honed by years of fieldwork in every hellhole on Earth, his intuition sounded a serious alarm. Garen apparently believed Chen was dead. Had this woman really killed him? Was that why things were turning to shit?

"Where are we going?" The woman's voice was low, musical, and very strained.

"To a place that rents private jets. We are leaving for New York in about forty minutes."

"But... But I need to go home." Hysteria danced beneath her words.

Lars laid a hand over one of hers. "We can talk in the plane. Not here."

"New York?" The cabbie sounded ecstatic. "Hey, take me with you."

"Next time." Lars scanned neon marquees and located Ermstatter. "Right there." He tapped the cabbie's shoulder and pointed.

"I know where it is." The man sounded aggrieved and pulled the taxi to a crooked stop near the curb.

Lars got out, handed money to the driver, and gathered his things. He herded the woman and her suitcase toward the swinging glass door. Before he pulled the door open, he bent low. "You do have a passport?" She nodded. "Now would be a good time to get it out." She rifled through her purse and withdrew an Irish passport, with its red cover. He snapped it out of her hand and opened it. "Tamara MacBride from Dublin."

She nodded and yanked her passport back.

"Nice to meet you, Tamara. My name is Lars." He bowed slightly.

"Sure and I don't know yet whether it's a pleasure or not."

Her voice carried the lilt of Ireland. It still trembled, but she didn't look quite as terrified as when he'd hauled her out of the taxi. Even frightened half out of her wits, she was still a striking creature. He wanted to crush her to him, bury his mouth in her hair, kiss her full lips, and tell her everything would be all right.

Not now. Not the time, he chided himself. *I am not even sure which side she is on.*

"Do not say anything inside the terminal," he instructed. "Just show the customs agent your passport when he asks for it. I will be busy for a bit signing paperwork for our airplane."

"Y-you can fly?"

"*Ja.* No worries, fair *fraulein.* I will take good care of you." He opened the door and herded her inside.

TAMARA STOOD off to one side as Lars signed sheet after sheet of paper at the counter. How was it even possible the man from the casino had rescued her? There was much more at work here than coincidence, and she wished to hell she knew what it was. Trying to appear nonchalant, she eyed him warily and tried to figure out what to do. Odds were good he was one of Jaret's men, but she'd never met him before. Never laid eyes on him before earlier tonight. Death had stalked her since she left the hotel. Was Lars just one more manifestation of it? He'd said he wasn't on *their side*, but he might've lied to pressure her into coming with him.

She shook her head, disturbed her brain felt like warmed over mush. The adrenaline surge from killing Jaret had long since subsided, leaving her dragged out and not functioning on all cylinders. Tamara forced herself to focus. Whatever this Ermstatter operation did, they certainly weren't busy. Two women tag-teamed, keeping paper flowing beneath Lars' pen. A customs agent came over to her and stamped her passport after asking her a bunch of questions.

Too nervous to sit, she shifted her weight from foot to foot. She still wasn't certain quite what had happened. They'd been nearly to the airport terminal, the driver slowing the cab preparatory to dropping her off, when she heard muted pops from a silenced gun. At first she thought she'd imagined it. The only place she'd ever heard a sound like that was on the telly or in the movies. She'd told herself her imagination was working overtime, that she was safe. She'd made the airport…

The night was warm, so the driver's window had been open. He'd made a choking sound, slumped over the wheel, and the cab had jumped the curb. Truth slapped her hard then. Too frightened to do anything but cower, especially after she saw two men racing toward her out of the corners of her eyes, Tamara had tensed, expecting another bullet to plow into her. Worse, her cat wanted out. Keeping it harnessed became a huge struggle.

Next thing she knew, Lars was there, dragging her out of the backseat…

"Fraulein?"

She hadn't heard him move to her side. Tamara squared her shoulders and looked at him. "Yes."

"We are ready. I called you from across the terminal, but you did not respond."

"Oh. Sorry." She sounded surly, but part of her still thought she should make a run for it.

Where would I go? How can I lose myself so Jaret's men won't be able to find me?

Desperate for information, she risked a sliver of shifter magic and directed it right at Lars. It pinged back clean. His eyes, which were focused on her, widened fractionally. Odd. He shouldn't have felt her appraisal, but it made her feel confident enough to not bolt into the night. She might be wrong, but he didn't feel like one of the bad guys.

"Follow me."

He led her through double glass doors that required a security code, and out onto the tarmac. A gleaming silver twin engine jet waited. He motioned her up its stairway, followed after, and told her to sit where she wanted. "I need to help the copilot get us airborne," he explained. "Once that is done, I will come back to the cabin to talk with you. The head is there." He gestured toward the bathroom. "A well-stocked kitchen is across from it." He swung his arm and pointed at a bank of built-ins. "Feel free to move about the cabin once I tell you we have reached cruising altitude."

She giggled, and then clapped a hand over her mouth. "Sorry. Sure and nothing is funny, except you sounded just like a stewardess on a normal flight."

He smiled. It lightened the severe planes of his face and made him extraordinarily handsome with his ice-blond hair and gray eyes. "We aim to please, *fraulein*. Relax and enjoy the flight." He tucked a cell phone into what looked like a computer case and drew out a larger item. A satellite phone, which he clipped to his belt.

Worry fluttered in her belly. What did she really know about this man, other than he'd coincidentally been in the right place at the right time? "Um, I didn't think you could use phones in flight."

He nodded. "That is true for passengers on commercial flights, but not for the reasons you might think. Cell phones that are visible to too many towers will not work, but even the smaller private planes frequently have sat phones in them."

She snorted. In spite of strong reservations, she found herself relaxing a little. Something about Lars was hard to resist, and she appreciated him taking the time to answer what must've seemed like a stupid question.

"I have a feeling traveling this way will spoil me forever."

His grin broadened. "It will. No maybe about it. I still fly commercially, but only when there is no other choice." Brushing past her, he hurried to the front of the plane and disappeared behind a door that closed behind him.

Tamara took off her jacket, settled onto a plush settee, and buckled her seatbelt. Her body felt electric where he'd touched her. She remembered her graphic sexual fantasies of him, and her face heated. The plane taxied, and then rose smoothly into the air. She peeked out a window and saw dawn lightening the eastern sky.

What have I gotten myself into?

Sure and I guess I'll find out soon enough, a pragmatic inner voice answered.

She closed her eyes, battling waves of weariness.

～

"*Fraulein*." Warm, sweet-smelling breath bathed her ear.

"I must have drifted off." She opened her eyes. Lars sat next to her. How long had he been there?

"Would you like something to eat or drink?"

"Sure. Anything." She yawned. "I'm going to wash my face and hands."

"By the time you get back, I will have prepared something for us. I suspect it has been nearly as long a night for you as it has been for me."

Darling, you don't know the half of it.

She undid her seatbelt and walked to the rear of the cabin and the small, neat head. Now that she wasn't running on sheer nerves, she was intrigued by what Lars had to say and curious why he'd rescued her. He'd mentioned earlier they needed to talk. She grinned at her reflection in the small mirror and finger-combed her hair. Next she held the water spigot open with one hand, bent over the stainless steel bowl, and splashed water on her face with the other.

"Talk away," she murmured, drying her face and hands with a paper towel. "I'll be all ears." It made no sense, but she thought she could listen to whatever he had to say forever.

CHAPTER 4

*L*ars busied himself in the galley arranging sliced cheese, crackers, and grapes on two Lexan plates. He was grateful for something to do. Tamara quite took his breath away. He wasn't positive, but what she'd scanned him with in Ermstatter's reception area felt a lot like shifter magic.

I only want it to be, he lectured himself, aware how lonely he was.

Though he'd shielded himself from the truth of it, Miranda choosing Garen had been one more nail in the coffin closing him off from a world of loving couples. He knew he appealed to women, but his profession—and his shifter blood—kept him aloof. It had never felt fair to open his heart too far—or encourage a woman to fall in love with him—when he had so many secrets to keep.

It was why Miranda would've been such a good choice. An espionage agent and shifter herself, she would have understood his needs perfectly. Despite lots of empty sex, he'd always known he could never seriously consider any woman other than a shifter for a permanent partner. Yes, Miranda had been ideal. More than ideal, actually.

Stop! She belongs to my closest friend.

The door to the head snicked open behind him, and Tamara

emerged. Spots of color splashed both cheeks, heightening her already-dramatic coloring. "Help you with those?" She arched a brow.

He handed one of the plates to her. "Unless you wish more than this, I am done. What would you like to drink?"

"Is there any juice, or mineral water?"

He opened the refrigerator and perused its contents. "Both."

She leaned so close, the warmth of her body seared him. Rather than asking, she reached around him and plucked a carton of vegetable juice blend from the center shelf. As quickly as she'd come up next to him, she was gone. Lars felt grateful she wasn't still hovering. Heat rose up his neck and swept over the top of his head. Selecting orange juice for himself, along with a bottle of water, he shut the fridge and took a steadying breath. He had to tamp down his attraction for her. It would only get in the way. For all he knew, she was in cahoots with Jaret Chen's gang. She'd certainly looked like Chen's woman in the casino.

Best tread carefully.

He pulled two napkins from a drawer, picked up his plate, and walked to where Tamara sat. She'd moved to one of the seating configurations where four seats faced one another, two on a side. He set his plate down and went back for his drinks. By the time he settled across from her, her plate was nearly empty. "Would you like more, *fraulein?*"

She shook her head. "I saw where things are. If I want anything else, I can get it myself. You surely don't have to be waiting on me."

He nodded, put a piece of cheese on a cracker, and ate it. Lars knew he was stalling, but he wasn't certain where to start. It wasn't as if she was his prisoner and he could fire questions at her willy-nilly. Tamara watched him with her sea-blue eyes over the top of her juice container. At least she'd regained her composure. Perhaps that might be a place to begin.

"You are looking more relaxed."

"Yes. Thank you." She licked her lips and set the juice aside. "Why were you in the casino?"

Lars bit back a laugh. "Direct. I like that in a woman. Funny, but that was one of the questions I planned to ask you."

She cocked her head to one side, regarding him intently. "You didn't exactly answer me."

Lars narrowed his eyes. "How about if we try a different topic? What is your connection to Jaret Chen?"

She studied her hands. Lars could almost feel her thinking, sorting through half-truths and discarding them. *"Fraulein."* He reached across the space between them and placed his index finger beneath her chin to tilt her head so she had to look at him. "It is better for you to remain silent than to weave fabrication. I will know if you are lying."

She drew back. "How?"

He shrugged. "How does anyone do anything? It is one of my…talents."

She dragged a breath deep into her lungs, blew it out, and did it again, but she didn't look away. "All right," she said after a space of time. "I was his girlfriend."

"Was?"

She nodded but didn't offer anything further. Lars let go of her chin. Where to go from here? "Did the two of you have a fight?"

"In a manner of speaking." Her tone was carefully neutral. "What happens after we get to New York?"

"You changed the subject."

She picked up a grape, popped it into her mouth, and chewed. "Is that against the rules?"

Lars' lips twitched. In addition to being stunning, Tamara had a quick mind. "How'd your taxi driver end up dead?"

"What is this? Twenty questions? Except neither of us answers any of them." She gave her head a little shake. It made the feathered ends of her hair dance around her high cheekbones. "I have no idea what happened. One minute we were almost to the airport. The next, the cab crawled over the curb and you showed up."

"That is not quite all, *fraulein*." Lars set his plate aside and moved to the seat next to her. "You were as frightened as anyone I have ever seen."

"Sure and wouldn't you have been?" she countered, drawing herself up straighter in her seat.

"Probably."

"Next you'll be telling me you're used to sharing cars with the dead."

"I am not certain anyone ever gets used to something like that."

He locked gazes with her, and almost wished he hadn't. Pools of blue light, her eyes drew him inexorably nearer. Without knowing quite why, he laid a hand on the side of her face. When she didn't pull away, he traced his fingertips over her full lips. She laid her hand over his. He thought he read invitation in her eyes and leaned closer. It wasn't a good idea; the sensible part of his mind argued against it—and lost. He replaced his fingers with his mouth. What began as the barest brushing of his mouth against hers turned into a heated kiss.

She opened her mouth to him, welcomed his tongue. He wrapped her in his arms and lost himself in a kiss that held desperation as much as attraction. His headset crackled. The copilot asked for something to eat and drink, or for him to come fly the plane for a bit so he could get his own snack.

Tamara drew away, her breath coming quickly. Her lips were swollen from their kiss, and color spilled across her face. "What was that about?"

"The other pilot." Lars touched his mouth to hers again briefly, aware he was achingly hard. He got to his feet, feeling torn. Part of him, the part belling out the front of his trousers, wanted to ravish the woman staring up at him. His rational side urged caution. He needed to know more, a whole lot more, before he held Tamara in his arms again. If the copilot hadn't disturbed them, he feared they'd have ended up coupling on one of the airplane's lush leather seats. As it was, the smell of their arousal hung heavy in the still cabin air.

"Where are you going?" Her voice was low, husky. Her nipples were clearly outlined beneath her sweater, as were the curves of her obviously braless breasts.

"To take care of the airplane," he said tersely. "I will see you later."

TAMARA WATCHED his tightly-muscled body stride up the aisle toward the cockpit. She shivered slightly. Because she hadn't wanted to answer any of his questions, she'd invited the kiss that had turned into something so amazing, she still couldn't quite believe it. His scent—musk and bay rum—clung to her. If she closed her eyes, she could pretend he was still close.

The cockpit door opened. Hope flared, but it was the other pilot, the one she hadn't spoken with. Short, rotund, and bald, he favored her with a nod before disappearing into the head. When he came out, he tossed some snacks into a plastic bag and loped back up the aisle.

Tamara waited. Surely Lars would rejoin her, but minutes ticked by and he didn't.

Who am I trying to kid? He probably has either a wife, or a girlfriend, maybe both.

A familiar sadness filled her. A man who was that handsome couldn't possibly not be spoken for. Even if he were free, there was the little problem of her shifter blood. Lars was gorgeous and hot, but definitely not for her.

"What will I do once I get to New York?" she muttered.

It was an enormous city and as good a place as any to be anonymous. She'd have to work. Maybe she'd look up the few magazines she'd freelanced for. They might have an assignment or two to keep food on her table. One thing for certain, she couldn't tell her family anything. Or anyone else, either. She hated to hurt them, but knowledge of her whereabouts would probably place them in grave danger.

Jaret's drug cartel had a long reach. It was possible no one would miss him, or want to avenge him, which might mean she could return to Ireland someday…

Dream on, sister. It certainly isn't looking like that right now.

She hadn't said anything to Lars about the two men racing toward the cab just before she froze into a fetal position in the back seat. Had he seen them too? One thing was certain. If he hadn't shown up, she had no doubt the men would've jumped in and taken off.

Would I have had the presence of mind to leap out? To scream my head off?

She bit her bottom lip. Those were simple questions. She should be able to answer them but couldn't. Not with any level of confidence. If she'd been capable of either of those things, she'd probably have done them before Lars dragged her quaking body out of the cab.

Maybe she could tell him part of the truth. That she'd returned to her room to find Jaret already dead. Not knowing what else to do, she panicked and fled. Tamara rolled varying combinations of words around in her mind. Only a few phrases constituted a bald-faced lie. Despite what Lars had said, no one could determine if she wasn't quite telling the whole truth.

She stood and walked to the cockpit door, raised her fist to knock, and then dropped it to her side. She laid an ear next to the door and dialed in her mountain cat senses. The low hum of conversation filled her augmented hearing. Unfortunately, the men spoke German. Not one of her languages. Now if it had been French, Greek, Irish, or Italian, she'd have been home free.

Damn!

She made her way back to the settee where she'd started out and shrugged her jacket over her sweater. Lars had said he'd *see her later,* whatever that meant. She assumed he'd return to talk with her, but he didn't appear to be in any big rush. If he felt guilty about kissing her, because he'd been unfaithful to someone, she could let him know she didn't hold any expectations on account of that kiss.

That's it. I'll make it clear I need a friend, not a lover. Maybe he'll know somewhere in New York I can stay for a few nights, just until I get my bearings.

LARS SWIVELED his body to get his legs away from the rudder pedals and stretched them. A few moments before he'd heard Tamara right outside the cockpit door. When she didn't knock, he'd tensed. What did she want? Was she part of the group trying to get rid of him?

He stood and walked to the door, sniffing for the telltale odor of explosives. It wasn't likely, but he had to check. If the plane exploded, she'd die right along with him and the other pilot.

"Was machst du?" the copilot asked.

"Nothing." A bit more confident, Lars cracked the door. All he smelled was her earthy scent, full of jasmine and lilacs. He shut the door, feeling ridiculously pleased. She'd wanted to talk with him but had chickened out. Maybe that meant…

Stop. It means nothing.

He returned to his seat and scanned his instrument cluster. It was still an hour before they'd land. His satellite phone vibrated against his side. Lars pulled it out and punched *Answer*.

"Ermstatter told me you have a woman with you," Garen said, not bothering to start with *hello*. "Who is she?"

Lars glanced at the copilot. "Would you mind?" He pointed to his phone.

The taciturn man actually smiled. "Not at all. I'd welcome a break. I'll return before we enter our final approach to land." He glanced at his watch. "That should give you about half an hour."

"Thanks." Lars waited until the copilot left and the door locked automatically behind him. He could use the numeric code panel to return to the cockpit. Lars shifted his attention to Garen. "There is much you do not know."

"I'm listening. Talk fast. These satellite calls cost an arm and a leg."

Lars was just finishing when Garen broke in. "This line's as scrambled as I can make it. Chen is dead. At first they suspected you, but you're in the clear. Scuttlebutt, at least from his people, is the woman did him."

Even though he'd suspected as much, breath whooshed out of Lars. "She does not seem the type," he stammered.

"I didn't know hit people had a *type*," Garen said dryly.

"No wonder they tried to kill her at the airport." Lars closed his teeth over his bottom lip, thinking.

"I did a little more research just now, once I had your passenger's name," Garen went on. "Tamara's sister was Chen's woman. She died of a drug overdose about eight months ago."

Puzzle bits ticked into place. Tamara must've avenged her sister's death. "I cannot just turn her loose in New York," Lars muttered. "Chen's gang will find her, kill her."

"Have you talked with her about any of this?"

"I tried—"

"It speaks well of her that she had the presence of mind to keep her mouth shut."

"Christ! Stop interrupting me!" Lars tightened his hand on the yoke. The plane shuddered before stabilizing.

"We could use her," Garen said flatly. "Sounds like she'd make a good agent."

"Do you have reason to believe she's a shifter?" Lars asked carefully. He tamped down wild hope racing through him.

"Maybe. Her sister was. So are others in her bloodline."

"Say more."

"I tracked her to one of two shifter families. She has to belong to one or the other."

"But that is marvelous news." Lars clamped his jaws together before something else slipped out.

Unfortunately, Garen had known him a long time. "Marvelous? Why do I get the impression this Tamara is a knockout?"

Lars snorted. "If you have done as much in the way of research as I suspect, you have already seen a photograph."

"Now that you mention it…" Garen drawled, letting his words dangle. "Bring her to Seattle. We can figure things out from here."

"What if she does not want to come?"

"Fuck her into insensibility. You can be downright irresistible when you put your mind to it."

A laugh bubbled up from his belly, followed by another. In moments, he was hooting with laughter, and relieved as hell no one could see him. When he could talk again, he said, "Thanks for the vote of confidence, old friend."

"Hey. Miranda even considered taking you for a roll in the hay, and she's quite discriminating."

"She told you that?" Incredulity was like a one-two punch after his bout of mirth.

"She tells me everything, just like you told her about you, me, and all those women we shared in some of the world's hellholes."

"Touché." Heat rushed upward from his chest. He had told Miranda a lot, way more than he should've. "Sorry. You were not mated then."

"Stand down. I'm not pissed. Let me know when you're airborne again and give me an ETA. I'll send a car and driver to meet you at Boeing Field."

Lars opened his mouth to reply, but Garen had disconnected. He reattached the sat phone to its belt clip and digested what he'd heard. It explained a lot. Tamara would've blamed the kingpin heroin dealer for her sister's death. He set his mouth in a firm line. Too bad about that. It must've been hell having a family member who was an addict. He couldn't even imagine the heartache something like that would cause.

It was incredibly gutsy of Tamara to put herself in the line of fire to avenge her sister's death. She must've been a hell of an actress to deceive someone like Jaret Chen. Rumor had it he was an addict, but he ran a damned tight ship.

Handy that he's dead. Makes my life easier.

The cockpit door creaked open, and the copilot got back into his seat. "Did you call the tower?"

"I was just getting ready to do that." Lars keyed his mike and relayed their position to JFK. The air traffic controller fed him a list of instructions, which he jotted down.

The copilot held out a hand. Lars handed him the list, and the copilot fed data into the onboard computer system. "How is our passenger?" Lars asked carefully.

"Napping." The copilot looked up and winked. "Quite the looker. Friend of yours?"

Lars made a noncommittal gesture. "Are you returning to Nice immediately?"

The copilot nodded. "Yes, but not the way you might expect. Ermstatter made me reservations on Swissair. I'll be cutting it close because we had more of a headwind than I'd anticipated. Could you take care of buttoning up the plane?"

"Of course. I am surprised you would not want to stick around to fly it back to Nice."

"I do as instructed. I was told your employer would take care of returning our aircraft and that you will be continuing in this same plane to your final destination."

Lars blew out a pleased breath. As usual, lady luck was with him. His life would be much simpler without the copilot hanging around. It would make it easier to have a frank discussion with Tamara. FAA regulations aside, he didn't need a second pilot to fly the plane. Now if he could just clear New York without anyone bothering him about that little detail, life would truly be sweet.

CHAPTER 5

Tamara feigned sleep because she didn't want to have to make small talk with the other pilot. Once he went back into the cockpit, she straightened in her seat and looked outside. They'd backtracked through dawn across the Atlantic, and the sky along the eastern seaboard was just pinking with the first rays of today's sun. She buckled her seatbelt and readied herself. The plane cut smoothly through the air, landed with barely a shudder, and taxied into an enormous hangar. Once they came to a stop, she got to her feet.

The cockpit door opened and the copilot rushed past her, flight bag in one hand and a garment bag slung over his arm. "Hope you had a nice flight," he called over one shoulder and popped the rear door. She stared after him. Should she follow? Tamara took a few tentative steps toward the plane's open hatch.

"*Fraulein*," Lars called from the cockpit. His voice was so clear it took her a moment to realize the copilot had left the door open. "Wait, if you please. I must shut things down here, and then I will assist you."

She looked longingly at the cockpit door, wanting to spend more time with Lars, even if it was only walking from here to customs.

I'm being ridiculous—and pathetic. I can take care of myself. It's best for everyone if I leave now, wend my way through the customs line on my own...

"Sure and I'll be all right," she called back. "Thank you so much for your kindness."

Lars exploded through the cockpit door. "Do not leave. It is not safe. I have five more minutes work."

"What do you mean not safe?" she sputtered. "I just arrived. Surely no one could possibly know—"

In lieu of an answer, he grasped her wrist and pulled her down the plane's aisle after him. Back in the cockpit, he sank into a plushy, padded seat after pushing her into the other one.

Tamara gaped at the array of instrumentation. The entire dashboard, and much of the plane's ceiling, was covered with round displays, square displays, levers, dials, and everything in-between. "By all the blessed saints." She tapped a few of the displays and shook her head. "How do you keep them straight?"

He interrupted clicking things off, and making notations in a leather-bound notebook, long enough to look at her. "You should see the large, commercial jets. They have many more controls. There." He got to his feet. "We can leave now. I will instruct a flight crew to have the plane ready for us. We depart in eight hours."

His words hit home. "We?" She squeaked the word out. "What are you meaning by *we*? I must find my own way. I can't let you—"

"Ssht. Enough." He set his jaw in a hard line and nudged her back into the cabin.

She walked to where she'd left her suitcase, hefted it, and tried again. "Like I started to say earlier, thank you kindly. Might you have any idea where I could stay in this city?"

He nodded curtly, dropped the satellite phone into his computer case, and picked up his two bags. "We can discuss that—and other things as well—once we have cleared customs."

"Sure and we can be discussing it." Concern warred with her better judgment. "Why are you believing I'm still in danger?"

"We need privacy for that conversation, *fraulein*. It will occur once we have finished with customs."

He sounded so distant, so formal, she stared at him. Was this the man who'd been within a hairsbreadth of laying her on the plane's floor and making love to her?

Maybe he really does have a wife.

She cleared her throat to mask her discomfiture. "How long will customs take?"

"Depends how busy they are this morning. Generally, the private plane passengers receive preferential treatment."

A uniformed man appeared in the plane's rear door. "Welcome to the U S of A," he said, sounding more fatigued than jovial. "When will you require the plane again, sir?"

Lars glanced at what appeared to be a very expensive wristwatch. "It is nearly six thirty a.m. Shall we say between four and five this afternoon?"

"Which would you prefer, sir?"

"We can split the difference. Have her prepared to roll at four thirty."

"You got it. Are you and the lady ready to deplane?"

Lars quirked an eyebrow at her. Tamara nodded. The man stepped aside, and she walked down the stairs and into an enormous hangar. She turned to Lars, who was right behind her. "Why are we inside?"

"It is better for the airplanes to be out of the weather, but the real reason is it allows customs to search for contraband, and lessens the odds of someone smuggling anything into the country."

She glanced about. "Where do we go?"

He pointed and then placed a hand beneath her elbow. "Last door at the end of the hangar."

Customs went as smoothly as everything else. Lars hadn't been joking when he'd told her flying this way would spoil her forever. "What's next?" she asked.

"Follow me."

They took an elevator to a well-appointed, private lounge with a killer view of the runway. He held a brief discussion with a young blonde woman behind a counter before joining her. "I have rented us a small suite for the day. My company has an apartment in the city, but I do not wish to take the time to travel to it." His gray gaze bored into her. "Does that meet with your approval?"

"I guess so." She pursed her lips together. "I still think…" He laid a hand over her mouth, forestalling the rest of her words. "Now you look here." She drew away and kept her voice low. "You cannot be treating me as if I were a child."

He bent close and spoke near her ear. "Please, *fraulein*. We do not want to draw attention to ourselves. Our rooms are very close. Just down that hallway."

She took a measured breath. If he hadn't tossed in that bit about her being in danger, she would've picked up her suitcase and lost herself in the crowd. As it was, maybe she should hang around long enough to see what he knew. She'd been assessing him surreptitiously while he spoke to the blonde, and his insistence that she stay didn't feel like a trap. Sincerity all but shimmered from him.

"All right." She jerked her chin upward. "Lead out."

His relief was palpable. He held the door of the lounge open and ushered her down a long hallway, up a half flight of stairs, and to a door marked 15-C. After a momentary grapple, he pulled an electronic key card from an inner jacket pocket and swiped it across a panel next to the door.

She stepped through once the door swung inward, and her jaw fell open. She wasn't certain what she'd expected, but the well-appointed suite laid out before her rivaled her accommodations in Monte Carlo. Beige and off-white sofas with plump, colorful cushions were arranged around a big screen television. A small kitchen sat off to one side with stainless steel appliances and a rectangular table. Across from the kitchen were two closed doors, presumably a bedroom and bath.

She dropped her suitcase and purse, and spun to face Lars, who had just closed the suite's door and activated the deadbolt. "Tell me about the danger. Now."

"Would you care for something to eat or drink?" He divested himself of his valise and computer bag, tossing both onto the floor near a coffee table.

"No. The sooner you tell me what you know, the sooner I can figure out how I'm going to survive here."

LARS SWALLOWED. He'd spent the last half hour of the flight considering how to approach Tamara. Blurting out that he thought she'd killed Jaret would probably be a mistake since she was still skittish enough to bolt.

"Well?" She tapped one foot impatiently and settled her hands on her hips. "Did you lie about me being in danger? How would you have found out about something like that?"

"No, *fraulein*. I did not lie. This conversation might go better if we were more comfortable." He settled on one of the sofas and patted the spot next to him.

She started his way, and then veered off and sat on the sofa at right-angles to his. "Okay," she said through tight lips. "I'm comfortable enough."

She wasn't going to make this easy. Lars steepled his fingers together, surprised by how sweaty his palms were. He'd faced down seasoned killers with more aplomb than he felt right now. "I work for an organization that makes it their business to know things. While we were airborne, one of my associates called. Ermstatter told him you were on the plane, and he wanted to know who you were. Once I told him, he did some research through an extensive computer network."

Her eyes widened, and she drew into herself like a puppy that had been kicked. Lars extended a hand toward her and hastened on.

"You have nothing to fear from us. Earlier you asked why I was in the casino. I was tracking Jaret Chen. It probably will not surprise you to know he is dead." Lars sent his shifter magic outward, casting it in a net to assess both her reaction and the truth of her next words.

She sucked in a shaky breath and kept her gaze on the floor. "I found him that way in our rooms. I was afraid—" her voice trembled "—so I ran."

Lars felt her lie in the pit of his stomach, but didn't confront it directly. "I also know about your sister and her drug problem. I am so sorry for your loss."

Tamara looked at him out of blue eyes that held a haunted edge. "Moira never used drugs," she said, a hard edge of defensiveness roughening her voice. "That animal killed her and made it look like an overdose."

"All the more reason you would have wanted him dead." Lars kept his voice low, gentle. "I am no stranger to killing, *fraulein*. Some people are so bad they deserve their fate."

"Oh." Her voice was desolate, broken. "I'm guessing you know, then, or you wouldn't have said that bit about bad people."

"*Ja*. I know. It takes much courage to—"

A rush of unintelligible words in Irish tumbled from her, drowning out the rest of his sentence. Her eyes filled with tears and overflowed. She ignored the flood. "Y-you won't be telling anyone," she moaned and wrapped her arms around herself as if she'd never get warm again. "Oh dear God, you said one of your associates knows too."

Lars couldn't stand to see her suffer. He moved to her side and took her into his arms. She sobbed against him while he smoothed her hair and waited for the storm to subside. "You need not worry about my associate, Garen, or myself. Or any who work for my firm, Rubicon International. What we, yes, *we*, must concern ourselves with is that Jaret Chen's gang has apparently decided you killed him. It is why they came after your taxi—and why they did not bother me again after accosting me on my way to the airport. I thought it curious at the time that they did not send another agent after my car, or simply shoot the tires out, but now I understand why they left me alone."

She pulled away from his chest and snuffled, wiping her sleeve across her face. Lars handed her a handkerchief from one of his many pockets, and she blew her nose. "What was I supposed to do?" she demanded. "He killed my only sister. I'm certain of it, though I don't have the kind of proof a magistrate would want. Moira's death nearly killed our da. My family will never be the same."

"You do not have to justify yourself." Lars held her gaze. "I had planned for Jaret to meet with an...untimely accident. It is why I was in Monte Carlo. I owe you a debt, since you did my job for me."

Tamara sucked in a surprised breath. "Y-you work as a...an..." Her voice ran down. She couldn't get the word out.

"I work in international espionage," he said smoothly. "Many activities comprise my line of work."

"Oh." She glanced down. "Maybe I'll be wanting something to drink after all."

"Of course." He stood and strode to the kitchen, where he took a quick inventory. "It appears we have juice, mineral water, beer, and quite the selection of wine and hard liquor."

"Is there any Irish whiskey?"

He chuckled. "Of course, *fraulein*." Lars plucked a small, sealed bottle from its shelf, found a shot glass in the cupboard, and returned to Tamara.

She ignored the shot glass, twisted the top off the liquor bottle, and drained half of it. "Whew. Burns." She shook her head. "It's actually a relief someone knows," she blurted. "Makes it seem less hideous, somehow."

"I understand." He sat next to her again and opened his arms. After a hesitation, she allowed him to hold her. "Let me tell you a story, *fraulein*."

"Sure and I'd like that. It will give me something else to think about."

Lars nodded to himself. That was his intent, to normalize what she'd done and help her come to terms with it. He wouldn't bother to mention that the story he was about to tell had happened almost three hundred years before.

He tightened his hold on her and began to talk. "When I was much younger, I was involved in a…situation. I had business in a bank in Heidelberg. My friend, Garen, met me at the bank because he and I had made plans to have supper together. He was waiting for me to finish with a certain financial affair when a thief entered the bank, intent on getting as much money as he could. Garen has an almost psychic side. He intuited what the man was about, even before he approached the counter with his demand, and jumped him. They rolled about on the floor. Garen was shot."

Lars stopped to take a breath. "I was seated at a desk off to one side. I dove on top of the man and strangled him, worried all the while about who was attending to Garen. As soon as I could, I scooped my friend up and carried him to…where he could get help."

"He survived because of you." Tamara's voice was muffled against his chest.

"Yes, *liebchen*, he did." Lars buried his hands in her hair. "That was the first man I ever killed, and I have never forgotten how it felt."

She shifted her position in his arms and wove hers around him, talking against his chest. "Jaret was pretty stoned out on heroin, but he woke up after I stabbed him and came after me." Her body shuddered in Lars' arms. "I was so scared, but I just kept stabbing him until he didn't move anymore."

"You used a knife?" Lars couldn't keep surprise out of his voice. "Such a personal way to kill. I would have thought a silenced gun much easier."

"And where would I have gotten one of those?"
Good point.

Lars chose his next words carefully. "Garen was impressed by your courage—and he did not even know about the knife. He and I assumed you had a gun. In any event, he wants to meet you. It is one excellent reason to come to Seattle with me later today. If things go well, there could be a job for you with Rubicon International."

She pulled away and looked at him. Her face was tear-splotched, but her beauty shone through and warmed his soul. "He wants to hire me to…uh, do what I did to Jaret?"

"It takes a long time to become a field agent—" he began.

"I'm thinking I'm not cut out for such things." She shook her head. "I'm a journalist. Sometimes I take pictures to go along with my articles. Before I left for Nice, I worked for the *Irish Times* freelancing."

Lars smiled. "Rubicon International could use a good PR person."

She smiled back. "That would be more to my liking." She looked at her lap. "Sure and I'm not certain why I had to avenge my sister. I just knew I'd not rest easy until her killer rotted in hell."

"I understand." Lars handed the whiskey bottle back to her, watching while she took another swallow.

She set the bottle down. "Yes, I'm thinking you do."

Lars traced the outline of her lips with a finger. He wanted her as badly as he'd ever wanted anything, but he could wait. They'd crossed an important barrier, and she was starting to trust him. It was as good a beginning as he could've hoped for. The shifter conversation could wait. So could undressing her and worshipping her body.

"I am going to take a shower, and then I must sleep for a few hours before I fly again."

"I wouldn't mind cleaning up as well." Color stained her cheeks. "If there aren't two beds in the bedroom, I can stretch out on the couch. I'm probably not as tired as you since I napped a little on the flight across the Atlantic." She captured his gaze with her own. "I don't quite know how to thank you. If you hadn't happened along, sure and I'd probably be dead now."

Good she understands that.

"No thanks needed, *fraulein*." He got to his feet before he crushed her to him and kissed her until neither of them could breathe. "Make yourself at home here." A thought occurred to him and he kicked himself for being sloppy. "You must have a cell phone." She nodded. "Give it to me."

She nodded her understanding, rose, and fished it out of her purse. "They can use it to trace where I am, huh?"

"Yes." He cracked the case, withdrew the sim card, and asked, "Do you still have the knife?"

"No. I cleaned it off and got rid of it in some thick bushes."

He nodded approvingly. "Excellent. I will be back in just a few minutes. Do not open the door under any circumstances."

He strode into the hall, annoyed he'd forgotten such a critical detail as her phone. Lars deployed shifter magic to scan for threats. "Thank God," he muttered when he didn't sense anyone anywhere close. He loped down the hall until he located a garbage chute. For good measure, he pulled everything electronic he could see out of the phone before he jettisoned the mess. Lars stared at the sim card. He started to chuck it after the rest of the phone, but had second thoughts. Best to destroy the damned thing. He reduced it to shards beneath his heel and tucked the pieces in a variety of spots between the garbage chute and his suite.

Reassured at least one problem wouldn't come back to bite them in the ass, he let himself back into the room. It would be a long eight hours. He wouldn't feel truly safe until they were airborne again.

CHAPTER 6

*T*amara made a full transit of the suite while Lars was gone. The bedroom contained an enormous bed. The bathroom was small, but did have a full-sized tub. A bath would be perfect, but she'd wait until Lars was done with his shower. A closet contained pillows and blankets. She'd just brought an armful of both items to the couch when Lars let himself back inside.

"You should take the bedroom," he said brusquely. "If there is trouble, it is better if I am close to the door."

Panic tightened her throat. She had to swallow before she could get any words out. "Do you think Jaret's men would try something here?"

Lars took a deep breath and smoothed the worry lines from his face. Tamara sensed he was about to whitewash things, so she moved until she was only a few inches from him. "Sure and you won't be needing to sugarcoat anything for me."

Grudging admiration darkened his eyes until they looked like a cloudy sky. "Jaret was highly placed in his organization, one of the leaders. These types of operations take retribution seriously. It is how they sustain so few casualties. They rule by fear."

"Will I ever be safe?" Her voice caught on the last word. A shudder ran down her back.

He placed a hand on her shoulder. "Not in the way you currently define the word, no." One corner of his mouth turned downward. "I have not been *safe* for years, *fraulein*. One learns to live with such things. Besides, safety is a carefully constructed illusion. None of us are truly safe—ever. An incompetent surgeon, a car with faulty brakes... Many things can cut a life short." He shrugged.

She clamped her jaws together to keep her mouth from trembling. It was obviously past time for her to grow up. "I guess I made my choice when I set my sights on Jaret."

"That you did, *fraulein*. There is no retreat from certain paths."

She felt the heat of him across the few inches that separated them. Her pulse quickened, but she resisted an impulse to close the distance and wrap her arms around his lithe, hard-muscled body. He didn't move; neither did she. He caressed her shoulder before turning abruptly.

Tamara pressed her lips together, lips that had been hoping for his mouth against them. If he had a wife, as she suspected, it was better to keep things clean and above-board.

"Open your eyes."

She snapped them open, not realizing she'd closed them, and gaped at a gun in the palm of his hand. "Have you ever shot one of these?"

She nodded. "Of course. In case you missed it, Northern Ireland has been a hotbed of terrorism for quite some time. The newspaper sent me there more often than I wanted." She plucked the revolver from his hand and examined it.

"Sit there." He pointed to a couch facing the suite's door. "If anyone enters the room, shoot them. This gun has a silencer, so it should not draw unwanted attention."

"But—"

"No buts. If it is housekeeping, they will knock and you will tell them to return later."

She swallowed hard and tried to establish détente with an altered world, one in which she was either a hunter or one of the hunted. "I understand."

And I surely wish I didn't.

She sat where he'd indicated and checked where the gun's safety catch was.

"I will not be long, *fraulein*. Once I have cleaned up, I will take over."

Nerves soured her stomach once he left her side. She heard water running in the bathroom, and the enormity of her situation set her teeth on edge.

Sure and what was I thinking? she lectured herself. *That I'd just do away with Jaret, fly back to Dublin, big as I please, and pick up the threads of my old life?*

She gripped the gun so tightly its plastic case left marks in her hand, and dunned herself for being a right fool. Blinded by outrage over Moira, she hadn't thought things through very carefully at all.

And now the chickens have come home to roost. All of them.

Tamara jolted upright at a sound from the hallway. She deployed her sensitive shifter hearing and listened intently. Silence, but it held an odd quality. As if someone was outside, trying to be quiet. She got to her feet and walked toward the door, gun at the ready.

There it was again. A muted scratching. Was someone trying to jimmy the lock mechanism?

What should I do?

Part of her wanted to open the door, shoot whoever was out there, and be done with things, but Lars had said not to open the door. She started toward the bathroom to talk with him. The scratchy noise intensified and she froze in her tracks. To her horror, the deadbolt snicked aside. Fighting her way past a sick sensation turning her gut to jelly, Tamara planted herself in a shooter's stance, feet apart, gun pointed dead at the door. Could she shoot someone point-blank that she'd never even met before?

"Sure and I guess I'm about to find out," she muttered.

The door blew inward. A woman stood in the doorway and Tamara's finger turned clumsy on the trigger, feeling like a stick of wood that wasn't connected to her body.

A young, attractive, woman dressed in blue jeans and a baggy sweater, with an oversized shoulder bag, stared at Tamara out of dark eyes. "What are you doing in here?" she demanded in a slightly accented voice. "This is my room. They just gave it to me downstairs."

"If that's the truth of things, show me your keycard." Tamara was proud her voice didn't quiver.

The woman dipped a hand into her shoulder bag. Tamara tensed, waiting. She instructed her finger to tighten around the trigger, but it refused to cooperate. Her brain shrieked at her to shoot the bitch, get it over with.

What if I'm wrong?

The woman had been fishing about in her bag for too long. Tamara bit her lip so hard she tasted blood and forced herself to fire. The woman must've sensed what was coming because she spun out of the way. Tamara fired again. The woman fired back, the sound muted from another obviously silenced weapon. Hot pain lanced through Tamara's shoulder.

The bathroom door slammed against its stops. Lars leapt through the air, tackled the woman, and drove her to the floor. Tamara raced to where they grappled with one another and stomped down hard on the woman's gun hand. With a muffled string of expletives in an Eastern European language Tamara didn't recognize, the woman's hand opened and Tamara snatched her gun.

Her shoulder was on fire. She bent to hold the gun to some part of the woman, any part, but Lars had his hands around her neck, choking her. "Shut the door," he gritted through clenched teeth.

When she got back to him, the woman lay in a limp heap. "Ach, Christ! Is she..."

"No. I could have killed her, but I did not. I do not wish problems with the authorities here. Nor do I want to be troubled with lengthy explanations that would oblige us to remain in New York."

Tamara rocked back on her heels and clamped a hand over her shoulder. In that moment, she realized Lars was naked and averted her gaze.

"You are injured." He jumped to his feet, strode to the bathroom, and dragged clothes and a towel into the living room. "Why did you not do as I instructed?" he growled as he dried himself and dressed.

"I was going to, but it was a woman." Tamara cringed. Her words sounded lame.

"Since when are women exempt from being assassins?" His tone dripped sarcasm. "How bad is your shoulder?"

"I have no idea." She tried for a dignity she was far from feeling. "It isn't like I get shot every day." She lurched upright, still holding her shoulder that burned with a life of its own.

He ran his sharp gaze over her, stepped to her side, and pried her hands off the wound. "Mmph. Looks like the bullet went through. You got lucky, *fraulein*. Let me take care of our guest here, and then I will do what I can for you."

"Won't I need a hospital?"

"Absolutely not. Too many questions for gunshot wounds. If we must, there are private doctors here in New York who will come to us."

"What are you going to do with her?" Tamara jerked her chin toward the comatose woman. Long brown hair spread around her where she lay on the floor.

"Better if you do not know." He thumped her chest with a finger. "If that fucking door opens again, I do not care if a ten-year-old is there, shoot to kill. Do you understand me?"

"Stop yelling at me."

He took a deep breath. "Sorry. I am angry at myself. I should have known better than to leave you alone."

She caught hold of her temper. It had always flared hot. "I'm sorry too. I didn't do what you said, but I promise I've learned my lesson."

His hard, flat gaze softened fractionally. He hefted the woman over one shoulder and let himself out the door. Tamara didn't need his instructions to lock it behind him.

She paced from one end of the suite to the other, gun gripped in her hand. It was the woman's gun, but since it was a 9mm, and had more stopping power than Lars' revolver, she clung to it. Adrenaline left an acrid taste in her mouth, and she felt light-headed. She told herself she wasn't badly wounded. Hadn't Lars said so? Despite efforts to soothe her frazzled nerves, her shifter side was frantic to heal the damage. If she changed to her cat form, the injury would repair itself quickly.

Why didn't I think of that the moment he left?

Tamara glanced nervously at the door, and then at the microwave oven's clock. She'd almost decided to shift and take care of herself when she caught her breath and slammed her palm against her forehead. How the hell would she explain her sudden recurrence of health? It wasn't as if she could tell Lars she'd found a faith healer lurking in the hall.

She licked at dry lips and sank onto one of the sofas. She only stayed for a moment before she got to her feet again, worried she'd bleed on the light beige upholstery. Stumbling slightly, she made her way to the kitchen sink, ran cold water, and drank from her cupped hands after she'd rinsed blood from them.

Panic swamped her when she understood she'd laid the gun on the kitchen counter. She gripped it again, water dribbling down her chin, and turned to face the door. It opened. Her hand tensed, finger tightening around the trigger.

"It is me, *fraulein*," Lars called before opening the door far enough for him to enter their suite.

Tamara dropped the gun back onto the ledge, buried her face in her hands, and burst into tears. She felt horrified by her lack of self-control, but couldn't stop sobbing. The harder she tried for composure, the worse things got.

Lars closed his arms around her. "There, there, *liebchen*. It will be all right. The woman will not bother us further. She will not wish to be found out, so when she regains consciousness, she will merely report back to her superiors. It will take her a while, though, since I removed her communications devices from her bag, along with her money, keys, and identification."

Tamara gulped air. "Who was she?"

"I have no idea. Her identification had to be falsified. No one in this business carries their true identity documents."

"Oh my God, sure and I was such a fool to let Jaret know who I was." Another sob pushed its way out, obliterating further speech.

Lars smoothed her hair back from her sweaty forehead. "Let me take a look at your shoulder." He let go of her and pushed her loose-necked sweater down. She grunted in pain while he probed from both sides with practiced fingers. "It is clean. The bullet went through muscle tissue. No vessels are torn, or you would be bleeding much more than you are."

She opened her mouth, and then shut it with a snap.

"What is it, *liebchen*? Do you wish a physician? He could disinfect and wrap it, plus antibiotics might be a good call. There is nothing magic about us leaving here at a set time."

Should I tell him?

She drew away and focused her gaze on the carpet. "I, er, um, that is, I can fix it myself, but I need privacy." She risked a glance his way, expecting to see horror—or pity—that she'd lost her mind. He just looked at her, his cool, gray gaze appraising.

"Would the bedroom do?"

She nodded. "This will sound odd, but no matter what you hear, don't come in." She offered a weak smile, but it faltered. "I have a feeling the lock wouldn't keep you out."

He did something curious then. He smiled. Really smiled, as if he hadn't a care in the world. It lightened his normally severe expression and turned him into rock star gorgeous. Lars half-bowed in her direction. "Take whatever time you need. I will watch over you—and honor your request for privacy."

"Don't... I mean aren't you going to ask me anything?" Tamara had prepared a half-baked tale about Irish witchcraft, but it didn't appear she'd need it.

"No. I am going to turn on the television and see if I can find a sporting match to watch."

It's almost like he knows.

He couldn't possibly. He's just being kind.

She wanted to ask a hundred questions, but there wasn't even one that wouldn't totally blow her secret side. Tamara walked across the room, her back very straight. She went into the bedroom and shut the door, taking care to engage the lock.

LARS WANTED to whoop and dance around the room, but he forced himself to turn on the television and flip through channels. Garen's intel had been right on. Tamara must be a shifter. If she summoned her animal form, she'd heal quickly. He pumped his fist in the air, and then jammed it over his mouth to stifle a triumphant laugh. Her hearing would be acute in her animal form. As a hedge, he turned up the television's volume.

This development would make the shifter conversation much easier, but there was no reason to have it quite yet. Tamara must be on sensory overload after everything she'd been through in just a few short hours. No point in making things any worse, or more difficult, for her. He wondered what she was. Wolves, bears, and mountain cats were most common, but he'd known coyote, bird, and even deer and elk shifters.

Deep in his computer bag, his cell phone jangled. Lars dove for it, but by the time he located it, it had quit ringing. He brought up his call log, but it said *private*, just like the last call to his phone. He punched one of the speed dial numbers, the one that would connect him to Garen.

"I just tried to reach you," Garen said.

"What? No hello, how are you, old friend?"

Garen snorted laughter. "My, you're sounding chipper, particularly since I just heard there was an attempt on your life, or the girl's anyway. It came in on my satellite feed."

"Our uninvited visitor, a woman by the way, was an amateur. The problem went away."

"A woman, eh?" Garen sounded interested.

"*Ja*. A Russian national from what I could tell, but her English was excellent."

"Humph. How's everything else?"

"Better than good, my friend. Tamara was shot, but she is closeted in the bedroom healing herself."

"Aha! Not that we have a corner on the magic market, but I was probably right about her being one of us. It makes things much easier. Did you talk with her about working for Rubicon International?"

Lars blew out a breath. "I broached the topic, but she has lived through a great deal in a short time. Things like this, well, they—"

"I'll have Miranda work on her when the two of you get here. It isn't as if we'd be sending her out on the front lines anytime soon."

An almost savage protectiveness surged, surprising Lars with its ferocity. "She has worked as a journalist. Surely we could use a decent PR person."

Garen laughed so hard, Lars held the phone away from his ear. Irritation tensed his jaw. A straight-shooter, Garen could be incredibly insensitive. When he could talk again, Garen said, "What we do doesn't generally require public relations. Aren't we usually flying beneath the radar?"

Lars chuckled, and his annoyance crumbled like over-baked bread. "It is only that I wish her to feel comfortable, safe."

"This is sounding serious, old friend. Is she that good in the sack?"

"I have not yet found out, but I am working on it."

"Maybe I should hang up. You can mosey on in there, shift, make a grab for her hot animal form—"

"No. Once we have coupled in both forms, we will be linked forever. You made that mistake with Miranda—before you discussed the ramifications. I wish to be more aboveboard."

"Aw, come on. I was more sloppy than shady."

"Whatever. I am fond of the fair *fraulein*. If we do make love, it will first be in our human forms. She does not know what I am, and I did not question her when she went into the bedroom alone."

"Playing it close to the cuff, eh?"

"Christ, Garen! In less than twenty-four hours, she has killed for the first time, been shot at, taken a bullet through her shoulder, and understands she is running for her life."

"You're probably right to ease into things." The teasing tone left Garen's voice. "You always did have excellent instincts. See you soon."

"*Ja*. Looking forward to it." Lars disconnected. Though his gaze settled on two nameless teams bouncing a basketball around a court, his mind was elsewhere. All he could see was Tamara, with her sea-blue eyes, shiny black hair, and pert smile.

His cock jumped to attention. Lars rearranged himself and let his fingers linger over his engorged shaft. He was imagining how her breasts would feel in his hands when the door to the bedroom creaked open. Lars grabbed an occasional pillow and dragged it into his lap to cover his erection. Embarrassment swamped him, but he tried for a nonchalant expression as Tamara, radiant and breath-stealing, stepped out of the bedroom.

CHAPTER 7

Senses still heightened from spending time in her cat form, Tamara scented Lars' arousal as soon as she cracked the bedroom door. It arrowed right to her crotch, which flooded with desire. Her face heated, and she knew she was blushing furiously. He gazed at her, his gray eyes smoky with something she didn't have a name for, looking like a human version of a big cat on the prowl.

"I heard the phone." Tamara ignored her suddenly heavy, aching breasts and the second heart beating between her legs.

"It was nothing." He shifted position on the sofa, and she noticed the pillow dead center in his lap. Had she interrupted him masturbating?

Her face got even hotter at the thought of his well-formed fingers stroking his shaft. Somehow she just knew his cock would be as amazing as the rest of him. She wanted to walk to the sofa, wrap her arms around him, and taste his lips again, but he wasn't exactly asking her to join him.

"Are you well, *fraulein?* Do you need me to find a physician after all?"

"Sure and I am mostly better. I worried the phone call might mean we had to leave, so I hurried things up a bit." She pressed her thighs together, not remembering if she'd ever been anywhere near this hot before.

"It was just Garen. His intel connections are excellent. He heard about the woman who tried to kill you and wished to assure himself we were all right."

"If that was all… I-I'll be bathing."

She tried to take a deep breath. It wasn't easy. At least in the bathroom, she'd escape the embarrassment of having walked in on him—and she could take care of her own needs. All she could think about was fucking Lars, feeling his hands moving over her body and his cock buried inside her. Before she tossed caution to the winds and threw her overheated body into his arms, she hustled into the bathroom. The second she shut the door, she crammed a hand between her legs and pushed her swollen labia against her fingers. Her other hand settled on a pebbled nipple. A muted yelp escaped, and she bit her lower lip to stifle further sounds.

A tap vibrated against the bathroom door. She froze. Had she flipped the lock? Tamara straightened. Another tap. "Yes?" Her voice rang hollowly. She dragged her hands away from her breast and pussy and stood straight.

"Open the door." Lars' voice was harsh, raspy with the same need raging in her nether regions.

Tamara snaked a hand out and turned the knob. He surged into the small space, crushed her against him, and slashed his mouth down on hers. She opened herself to him, desperate for the feel of him, the taste of him. His scent eddied about them. She inhaled hungrily, and the musk of his heat stoked her own inner fire. He sank his tongue inside her mouth. She sparred with it, nibbling, licking, sucking, biting. He ran his hands down her back and cupped the curves of her ass, drawing her against him. His cock pressed against her belly while he groaned and thrust against her.

She ground her hips against his pelvis and then moved to capture one of his legs between her thighs. The heat of his body pressing on her clit was almost more than she could stand. She reached between them and undid his belt and the fastenings on his trousers. Frantic to feel him, she pressed a hand inside his pants and curved her fingers around his cock. It was long, hard, thick, and quivering with need.

Her mind was a muddle. Shoes. His shoes would be a problem. She broke away from their kiss and slithered down his body until she knelt before him. Still gripping his shaft in one hand, she licked and kissed her way up and down it. He buried his hands in her hair and showed her the rhythm he needed. She milked him with hands, mouth, teeth, tongue. The hotter he got, the more she wanted to please him. All thoughts of removing his shoes, which was why she'd knelt in the first place, fled.

He tried to pull away, but she held fast. His cock bucked in her hand. He made an incredible sound, half purr, half growl, low in the back of his throat, just before semen jetted into her mouth. Tamara clung to him, made his pleasure last as long as it could.

He stroked her hair gently, murmuring in German. Even though his cock was still rigid, he pulled it out of her mouth, knelt beside her, and closed his mouth over hers. He dragged a couple of thick towels off a nearby rack, placed them on the floor and drew her down onto them. Next he tugged her sweater out of the way and settled a hand over one of her breasts. At first he just held its weight in his hand, and then he teased her nipple, twirling his fingers around it until it ached with desire. He trailed kisses down her neck, moved to her exposed breast, licked and suckled it thoroughly before exchanging it for the other one.

He fumbled with the button and zipper of her jeans. She pushed them down her hips. He moved lower, breath hot when his mouth moved across her stomach. She thrust her hips upward again and again, wanting to come, needing to come, wanting Lars to be the instrument that gave her body release.

He swirled his fingers around her clit and then moved his hand so he could sink two fingers inside her pussy. Heat seared her. His mouth. He licked, sucked, kissed her sensitive nub, while knowing fingers plumbed her vault. Tamara writhed beneath him. A climax spooled deep in her belly. He must have sensed it from the tension in her clit and against his fingers because he moved harder, faster.

She came, squirming and shrieking as spasms shot through her, but he didn't stop. A second orgasm crowded on the heels of the first, leaving her stunned, breathless.

Somehow, she found herself in his arms and held on like a drowning woman might to a spar. They lay like that for long moments as the world came back into focus. She remembered herself and struggled to sit. He let go and looked at her. Something flickered in the backs of his eyes. Was it sadness? Regret?

"I'm sorry," she murmured. "Sure and you're quite the attractive man. Everything has been so intense, I lost control of my judgment."

"Sex and death are linked, *fraulein*. Never forget that." His deep voice grated, full of strong emotion. "When one is close, the other is never far away. It is not accidental orgasm is called *la petite mort*. The little death. We never come so close to death as we do during sex."

"I hadn't heard that before."

Why wasn't he saying he liked her, wanted to get to know her better?

Och, and I forgot, he probably has a wife.

She got unsteadily to her feet and tugged her snug pants over her hips. "I'm sorry. I'll be keeping myself under better control."

He looked away. "As you wish, *fraulein*." He stood, gathered his trousers, zipped them, and bowed stiffly. "Thank you for a charming interlude." He turned and left, pulling the bathroom door shut behind him.

What the hell just happened?

She flipped the taps and started the tub filling. Tamara sat on the toilet and took off her lace-up boots. Next, she stripped off her clothes and got into the tub with a small bar of soap, a washcloth, and a miniature plastic bottle of shampoo. It was fortunate she had something to do that kept her rooted in the bathroom. She wanted to rush into the living room, strip him naked, and crawl all over his body. What they'd shared had been a teaser, an appetizer. She wanted more of him, much more.

"Back off," she murmured as she soaped, rinsed, shampooed. "If he were free, he'd have said as much." She snorted. He'd have said *something*. He certainly wouldn't have come up with that hokey lecture about sex and death. Never mind the philosophical yammering about orgasm. When she replayed their post-sex interaction, her inescapable conclusion was he'd seemed wretchedly uncomfortable.

Uncomfortable. Aye, that's the key. He wants me just as much as I want him. We caught each other at a weak moment. Now guilt's pricking him, on account of his wife or girlfriend, and he doesn't know quite which way to turn.

Tamara levered herself from the water using the sides of the tub. She stepped out and dried off, wishing she'd had the presence of mind to drag her suitcase into the bathroom. Now she'd have to crawl back into the same clothes she'd spent the last eight or nine hours wearing.

That's the least of my problems.

She opened the tub's drain, dressed, and hunted down a hairdryer. Tamara was stalling, but she wasn't anxious to leave the bathroom and face Lars. What on earth would they say to one another? Should she reassure him she wasn't a threat to his marriage?

I was going to do that earlier, and I never did.

She placed her hand on the doorknob and sought the same resolve that had strengthened her spine when things got dicey with Jaret. When she had her emotions well enough in hand to keep tears at bay, she took a deep breath. She'd always wanted a man just like Lars, but he was taken. Even if he wasn't, there was still the problem of her shifter blood. She'd just have to buck up and play the ball where it lay.

~

Lars stumbled from the bathroom. He hadn't meant to accost her, but he'd sensed her arousal when she stepped from the bedroom. His cock was already so hard it ached. Seeing her, knowing she struggled with wanting him, undid him. Once she'd opened the door—at his request—he'd been hit full on by the heady scent of her desire and the game had been up. Nothing shy of a tsunami crashing through the suite could have kept them out of one another's arms.

Ja and look what it has bought me. We grappled like animals on the bathroom floor. I did not even have the presence of mind to pick her up, carry her to the bed, make love to her like the princess she is.

Fury swept through him, and he pounded his fist into the nearest object. A lamp crashed to the floor. He froze, expecting the bathroom door to burst open, but then he realized she probably couldn't hear anything over the sound of running water. Blowing out a frustrated breath, he picked up the broken pieces and carried them to the kitchen wastebasket.

Because he felt too hyped up to sit, he ran cold water at the kitchen sink and sluiced it over his face. The sweet taste of her pussy lingered on his tongue. His cock twitched, wanting more —much more.

Her body was amazing, even better than he'd imagined. She had full breasts with sand dollar nipples the color of burnished copper. A light dusting of freckles covered her chest, making him suspect at least one of her parents was a redhead. A slender waist flared to generous hips and a firmly muscled bottom. Tight black curls guarded the entrance to her body. They'd glistened with her fluids even before he closed his mouth over her. And her legs… He shut his eyes for a moment, picturing them. Long and shapely, they were banded with lean muscle. She must be a runner, or a climber, to have legs like that. Or maybe she rode a bike.

He cursed softly in German. None of it mattered. He'd always been a klutz socially. Working as an espionage agent fit his makeup perfectly because he never had to make small talk or schmooze people. That was more Garen's job. Garen could be charming. Lars stumbled when he had to be anything less than straightforward.

He walked to a window, curled his hands around the sill, and looked out at the New York skyline. Forcing long, slow breaths, he catalogued what he knew about Tamara. It wasn't much. Really only what Garen had told him. Maybe if they got to know one another first… He shook his head. That wouldn't work. Not until the shifter stumbling block had been addressed. With that still standing in the way, the best they could tell each other would be half-truths.

He was three hundred sixty-seven years old, a few years older than Garen. Any history he shared with Tamara would be a sham unless he could admit that. He sensed she was much younger, but these things were difficult to assess.

Maybe I should not do anything until after we get to Seattle.

He winced. Definitely the coward's way out, but it seemed easier than any of the alternatives. What if she'd used some sort of Celtic witchcraft to heal herself and she wasn't a shifter after all? Garen's intel was good, but it wasn't foolproof. He hadn't gotten a look at her wound while they'd clawed at one another, ripe with need, because he'd never gotten her top off. All he'd done was shove it north of her breasts. If he'd seen her bare shoulder, he'd have recognized shifter healing. As it was, he could only guess.

I was little better than an animal in rut.

He let go of the windowsill, doubled his hand into a fist, and slammed it into his thigh. His muscles bunched like they did when he found himself in life-and-death situations, and he forced himself to relax, to breathe. He wouldn't do anyone any good if he was this spun out.

The bathroom door opened. Even though it was a normal sound, he started as if a gun had gone off behind him. The soft patter of her footsteps moved toward him. He arranged his face in what he hoped was a neutral expression and turned.

She gazed at him with a sad, drawn expression, and his heart shattered. Had he brought her to this? She'd been so strong, had survived her charade with Jaret Chen…

"*Fraulein*." He held out his hands.

"It's all right." She licked her lips. "Truly it is. I am sorry things got out of control. I assure you I won't be so brazen again." She looked at the floor. "Sure and I'm not understanding exactly what got into me, but I said that before."

"If that is what you wish," he said stiffly, not wanting to betray any emotion that she might construe as pressure to change her mind, "I, too, will be more circumspect. You are a very beautiful woman. Any man would—"

She shoved a hand toward him, palm facing outward. "Stop. It's better for us to speak of other things. How much more time until we return to the airplane?"

He glanced at his wrist. "A couple of hours."

She scrubbed the heels of her hands up her cheeks and blew out a breath. "Seems like enough time. Maybe you could be telling me more about this company of yours. The one you're wanting me to work for."

"What do you wish to know?"

She tried to smile, but it didn't reach her eyes. "Everything." Tamara walked into the small, open kitchen and began rifling through cupboards and drawers. "My goodness, but there's a decent selection of ingredients here. While you talk, I'll be making us a bit of a snack."

"*Ja*, the concierge sees these kitchens are well stocked. You do not have to cook for me, *fraulein*."

She spun to face him, her mouth set in a tense line, her eyes hooded. "I know, but I'm happier when I'm busy. If you see me reach for some ingredient you hate, speak up."

"I am easy to please. Whatever you prepare will be wonderful." Lars knew he sounded like an automaton, but his hands were tied. He couldn't talk about what he wanted to. There were too many barriers. He turned one of the kitchen chairs around and sat, crossing his arms over its backrest. Tamara moved about the kitchen with grace and confidence. She was apparently making an omelet-esque dish with chopped fresh vegetables and grated cheese. Because her back was to him, it spared them having to look at one another.

She'd asked about Rubicon International. What he could tell her about it was limited since he couldn't discuss its origins during the Revolutionary War, nor the fact that all field agents were shifters.

"Well?" She spoke to the skillet simmering in front of her, rather than to him. "It seems I have some decisions to make, and quite soon. I can't be making them without a spot more information."

"Of course, *fraulein*." Lars took a measured breath. "Garen and I founded Rubicon International when we became concerned about the incompetence of the United States government to deal with threats to the free world. It took many years, but we have gathered as fine a team of intelligence agents as exists anywhere. All our employees are loyal to the core. I head up the European headquarters and Garen the U.S. based one."

She set a steaming plate in front of him. It smelled wonderful and reminded him how long since he'd had a real meal.

"Would you like some tea with this—or maybe coffee?" she asked.

"Tea would be fine."

She nodded. "Excellent. I brewed a pot, and I made enough for both of us." She gave an apologetic shrug. "I suppose I should've asked, but I didn't want to be interrupting you."

"It is wonderful, *fraulein*. Thank you. Come sit so you can eat too."

She brought her own plate to the table, poured tea for them, and spread a selection of condiments in front of him. He looked up from eating. "This is exceptional. Have you ever worked as a cook?"

"Sure and I've done a little bit of everything over the years. Cooking, waitressing, receptionist work. My family wasn't exactly poor, but there was never much left over. I worked my way through college."

She tucked into her food. He watched her sidelong, thinking she was the most enchanting woman he'd ever met. Of course she wouldn't want a tongue-tied lout like him.

Tamara looked up. "Tell me more? How many people work for Rubicon International? Is it just you and Garen at the helm, or are there more executive staff?"

Lars nodded and took a sip of tea. It was brewed to perfection, just as the omelet was a succulent combination of crisp-tender vegetables, melted cheese, and just-right eggs. What a plus that she could cook.

A plus for some other man, he thought sourly.

He reined in his disappointment and addressed her questions. "Between the European firm and the American one, there are just over a hundred employees. All are independent contractors. A board of directors is in charge of operations, so there is not a boss *per se.* Garen, Miranda, myself, and two others comprise the board…"

She fed him questions so skillfully, Lars was surprised when he glanced over at the microwave's clock and discovered they'd run out of time. Even though they hadn't discussed anything of consequence, he felt better, more balanced, than he had while he'd watched her cook.

"Thank you," he said and got up. He gathered their few dishes and ferried them to the counter.

"Is it time?"

He nodded. "Yes, the airplane should be ready for us. I need to make a call and confirm our flight plan." He picked up his cell phone and started to dial when a thought occurred to him. "Not that anyone will ask, but if they do, you are my copilot."

Her eyes rounded. "I've fooled around a wee bit in single engine airplanes, but they're nothing like what we flew across the Atlantic.

I only recognized a few of the instruments in the cockpit. What if they ask for papers? A license?"

"They will not. If anyone should say anything, let me do the talking." He hesitated. "The basic flight principles are the same, no matter what the aircraft. Perhaps we could use the next few hours to augment your knowledge base."

A smile bloomed on her face, and she clapped her hands together. "Sure and I'd like that."

For the barest moment, she looked carefree. Lars wished he'd found her before she'd killed Jaret, wished he'd gotten to the man first. Though they hadn't talked about it, she was probably still figuring out her life would never be the same. That sort of thing sank in gradually. If she had to absorb the full impact of her actions all at once, it might be too much to take in.

He opened his mouth to give voice to some of his thoughts, changed his mind, and simply said, "My pleasure, *fraulein*." To avoid further conversation, he glanced at his phone and punched in the numbers to file their flight plan.

CHAPTER 8

Tamara settled into the copilot's seat and placed the headset Lars handed her over her head. Thank all the saints the tension had bled out of the air between them. Somewhere between her making them a midday meal and talking about his work, things had cleared. Maybe he'd found a place to stuff his guilt over being unfaithful. She covered a grimace with a cough and rotated her injured shoulder. Though she hadn't fully finished healing it in shifted form, it was good enough and the pain minimal.

He jabbered to the tower in pilot-ese, and the plane rolled out of the hangar and took its place in line for takeoff. "Do you have a private pilot's license?" he asked.

She nodded. "Yes, but not very many hours, and all of them in tiny, single engine planes."

"Why did you not fly more?"

"It's very dear. The only reason I learned to fly at all was because my brother owns a small air cargo operation just north of Dublin. He knew how much I loved being in the air, so he took pity on me. He couldn't afford to give me totally free lessons, but all I had to pay for was fuel."

Lars glanced at her and smiled. "I am so glad you love to fly. It is one of my passions."

Tamara couldn't help herself. The words burst from her before she could modulate them. "What are your other ones?"

Color rose from the open neck of his buff-colored linen shirt. Her headset crackled with a spate of instructions from the tower and he said, "They have cleared us for takeoff, *fraulein*. We will talk more once we are airborne. Place your feet on the rudders and your hands on the yoke. Feel what I do with them. Watch how I manipulate the throttle, and keep an eye on these sets of instruments."

He ran his index finger between two vertical rows, each studded with half a dozen round dials. They were identical, so one must be for each engine. He'd sidestepped her question about his passions, but there'd be time to ask again between now and Seattle.

She curled her hands around the yoke and settled her feet lightly on the rudder pedals. In an odd way, it almost felt as if he caressed her through the plane's controls. Tamara came close to laughing out loud at her wishful thinking. Powerful jet engines revved. The plane bounded down the runway and rose smoothly into the air. She felt when he let up on the right rudder pedal, felt when he evened out the yoke, watched the instrument display needles hover at the top of the green zone before settling back to where they had a larger safety margin. All the while, she eyed him sidelong through lowered lashes.

Lars flew the plane as if it was an extension of his body. He seemed to sense its needs in his bones, responding before the plane needed his intervention. He looked her way, caught her gaze on him, and hastily returned his attention to the instrument panel. Tamara looked away also, but his smoke-colored eyes remained in her mind. So did his thick, white-blonde hair and athlete's build.

"So." His voice sounded strained. "We have just passed through ten thousand feet. I understand you do not usually fly so high in the small planes without pressurized cabins, but what is important about ten thousand feet?"

She captured her lower lip between her teeth and tried to focus on something other than Lars' hands and wishing they were moving over her body rather than on the airplane's controls. "Takeoffs and landings are when the plane is vulnerable, in most danger of crashing." She took a breath, thinking. "With the small planes, it's a relief to get enough altitude so there's a cushion, in case I have to plan an emergency landing. I'm thinking it might be similar, but this plane is so heavy, if we lost power, surely we'd die."

He shook his head. "As I said earlier, the mechanics are the same. The more distance we are from the ground, the more time I have to come up with Plan B if something goes wrong." In a move that both shocked and thrilled her, he reached across the cockpit and placed a hand on her thigh. "Tell me about yourself, *fraulein*. I wish to get to know you."

Heat swooshed from her chest to the top of her head. "That doesn't sound like a flying lesson."

He cocked his head to one side. "The only things left to do are—" he held up one finger and tapped her thigh with it "—climb to cruising altitude and—" he held up a second finger "—set a course. They are the same as you already know." He tightened his fingers across the top of her thigh, stroking her. "I know this airplane. Let me get to know you."

Her crotch flooded with moisture, and breath clotted in her throat. Tamara struggled to understand how his touch affected her so strongly. She wriggled in her seat and clamped her legs together. "Sure and my life hasn't been very interesting—" she began.

He ignored her disclaimer. "Were you born in Dublin?"

"Yes. Well, not precisely. My family is from Drogheda, maybe fifty kilometers north of Dublin. It's on the River Boyne just before it runs into the Irish Sea."

"*Ja.*" His fingers inscribed small circles on top of her leg. "I know it. A port town. I spent time in Northern Ireland. We retreated to Drogheda by boat when things grew too dangerous."

Tamara twisted in her seat and gazed at him. "You've had quite the adventuresome life. Maybe you could be telling me about it, rather than my poor recitation."

He punched some numbers into the onboard navigation computer, and then turned and met her gaze. "There. We are at cruise altitude, and I have engaged the autopilot. I wish to get to know who you are, Tamara MacBride. I have had very little practice at this sort of thing, but you sharing what you want to about your life must be a first step. Otherwise, you will remain an enigma to me."

"Very little practice, is it? What about your wife?" she blurted.

He drew back as if she'd shot him. "Wife? What wife?"

"The one you were unfaithful to back in the airport terminal." She crossed her arms over her chest and glared at him. There. She'd gotten it out in the open. Maybe she hadn't been particularly elegant about it, but she'd become heartily sick of her cloak-and-dagger existence with Jaret.

A slow grin started with his mouth and finally reached his eyes. "I understand better now." He moved his hand from her leg to her crossed arms. "There is no wife. Not even a girlfriend. I have not led the sort of life that lends itself to emotional entanglements."

"Really?" Her voice came out as a squeak. She tried for composure, but made a grab for his hand and clung to it. She wanted to jump out of her seat and dance up and down the cockpit, but restrained herself.

"Really." Something warm and tender shaded his eyes to charcoal. "Now will you tell me about yourself?"

"Oh. Sure and I'd forgotten that was what began this."

His jaw tightened in what might have been resolve. "I did not mean for us to begin by pawing one another in that bathroom." He shrugged, looking sheepish. "You are a very beautiful woman. It was impossible to restrain myself once I knew you wanted me as desperately as I craved you." He squeezed her hand. "Who are you, *fraulein*? I assumed you were not married because no husband would ever agree to you posing as Jaret Chen's woman, but I wondered about a boyfriend, or maybe a fiancé back in Ireland."

"I've had both." She shook hair out of her eyes, still trying to wrap her mind around Lars not being attached. She'd thought it so many times, it had turned into reality.

"Start at the beginning," he suggested. "It is easier that way."

"I come from a big family. One sister, but you already know about poor Moira, and four brothers. I'm sort of in the middle of the pack. Mum and Da are still alive, and still married. They moved to the outskirts of Dublin before I started secondary school. Da is a jeweler and a better opportunity opened up for him. Mum plays violin; she got tapped by the Dublin Symphony soon after we moved."

Tamara considered what else she could share. Her entire family were shifters, but that part had no place here. It was also a reason Lars wouldn't be interested in her, and not something she could hide, at least not for very long. She clamped her jaws together, her earlier elation fading like a sunset gone bad. "This isn't a good idea."

"Why not?" He smiled encouragingly. "You were doing fine."

"I, er, that is, I'm not as free as I was thinking I was."

He knit his brows together. "Help me understand. That is not the type of thing one forgets."

"I can't talk about it." She let go of his hand as if it were a poisonous snake. "Maybe it would be a good idea for me to spend some time in the cabin." Unbuckling her seat harness, she stumbled through the cockpit door. Thank the bloody saints she made it all the way to the head before tears overcame her resolve not to break down. She closeted herself inside the tiny bathroom and dropped her head into her hands.

Maybe I should just tell him what I am.

But she knew she wouldn't because she couldn't stand to see the horror—or worse, pity—mirrored on his face when she revealed her true nature.

~

Lars retreated to his seat from where he'd been leaning halfway across the cockpit. He may not have had much experience with women, but Tamara's rapid about-face stunned him. Things had been going so well. She'd been warm, funny, half-aroused by his touch. And then it was as if a gateway had slammed shut.

What did I do?

He raked through his memory of what they'd said to one another and couldn't pinpoint a thing. To divert himself, he extracted data from the onboard computer. They'd be in the air for hours yet. Difficult hours if she remained in the cabin and refused to tell him what was wrong. He could leave the cockpit, but not for long. It was one of the disadvantages of not flying with a copilot.

Her scent lingered in the air. She hadn't been the only one aroused. His cock throbbed with need. He told it to stand down, but it had other ideas. Worse, as often happened when he was upset, his cat wanted out. He struggled to keep claws from bursting through his fingertips. Shifting in the cockpit was a terrible idea. His cat could do a lot of damage without meaning to.

He searched for a rational explanation. She'd been talking about her family when things had gone to hell. There had to be a connection, but what? He gripped the yoke so hard, the aircraft shuddered, and he forced himself to let go of the controls. The autopilot would take care of course corrections. He didn't need to do a thing until they got close to Seattle and Boeing Field.

Family. Was there something about her family she wanted to hide? He snapped his fingers. *Of course.* She held magic, probably shifter magic, but maybe something different. Magic always had a genetic basis, except for the odd lycan who acquired theirs through being bitten. She was protecting her family. Lars took a deep breath.

There wasn't any help for what would come next. He'd have to expose what he was. Maybe if he did, she wouldn't feel so vulnerable.

He unbuckled his seat harness, started to get up, and then stopped himself. What if she was so horrified by his revelation she came after him? Magic wielders danced to their own drummer, and they never worked with others outside their own ranks. He girded himself. If she was a witch or a Druid, and not a shifter, she might well decide he needed to die. It would be hard, but he prepared for the unpleasant task of taking her down for the duration of the flight —if she became unmanageable. There wasn't a doubt in his mind he could prevail in a direct contest.

She killed Jaret Chen.

Ja. But he was doped to the gills on heroin.

Lars scanned his instruments. Everything looked good. He stood and walked out of the cockpit. A cursory glance at the empty cabin told him Tamara had to be in the head. He strode down the aisle and tapped on the door. "*Fraulein.* Are you all right?"

"No." She sounded as if she'd been crying. "Leave me alone. Please."

"We are not done talking." He waited, but the door remained shut. He could've blasted through the lock with magic, but curbed his almost obsessive desire to hold her in his arms. The thought of her alone and distraught in the small head tangled his gut into knots.

Lars tried again. "Please, *fraulein.* I cannot remain out of the cockpit for long."

Moments passed. He'd almost decided to say what he needed through the door when the lock clicked and it opened. Tamara emerged, her face blotchy with tears. He held out his arms, but she shook her head.

"You'd best get back to the cockpit. I'll join you once I scare up a bottle of water."

Lars nodded. She looked so broken, so devastated, it took all his self-control not to draw her against him, but something in her eyes told him it wasn't a good idea.

She made shooing motions with both hands. "Get moving. I'll be there soon enough."

He walked the length of the plane, punched in the code, and reentered the cockpit. Lars shoved a small wooden block between the door and its frame to hold it open. He automatically checked his instruments to make certain the aircraft was still on course and the engines operating within parameters.

Tamara slid into her seat moments after he'd settled into his and buckled in. She looked pale, but determined, as she sipped a bottle of mineral water.

Lars' stomach was tight. He gauged the distance between them and left his seat harness unbuckled, in case she became uncontrollable and he had to launch countermeasures. This was one conversation Garen would never find out about. To discuss something so potentially volatile at thirty-five thousand feet was rash and irresponsible, but Lars couldn't wait until they landed. His heart ached; his soul felt empty.

He selected his words carefully. "I was surprised when you raced from the cockpit, so I have been trying to figure out if I said something that upset you."

"This isn't about you. It's about me. I-I can't talk about it. You've been more than kind. By all the blessed saints, you rescued me. I'd be lying dead on the streets of Nice if you hadn't stepped in."

"*Ja*, I know that part. Why did you leave as if demons dogged your heels?"

"I...can't talk about it." She repeated her earlier statement and set her water in a cup holder.

He nodded to himself. "Let me begin, then. You thought I was married. I am not. I know you have some type of magic. It is what you employed to heal your bullet wound."

He kept his eyes on her, watching intently for her reaction. She curled into herself and looked stricken.

"Sure and I canna talk about that, either." Her brogue got thicker. Her pupils dilated. She looked like a doe about to bolt from a hedge once she sensed a hunter.

"I will not hurt you, Tamara. Not now. Not ever. I understand about magic because I have some of my own."

She tensed and drew farther from him. Something flickered in the depths of her stricken eyes. Hope, or maybe fear. She didn't say anything, but a pulse quivered in her neck revealing a heart that beat too fast.

"Are you not interested in what kind of magic I hold?"

After a long pause, she nodded. Her knuckles whitened where she gripped the sides of her seat.

"If I tell you, will you trust me enough to tell me what is wrong?"

"Maybe." The word ripped from her throat and splatted against him. Glass shards couldn't have cut deeper.

He flinched. Her pain was raw, palpable, and it made his heart hurt. "You have no reason to trust me." He blew out a tense breath. The struggle with his cat was worsening. "Recognize I have no reason to trust you, either, but I am taking a huge chance by telling you this. I—" he swallowed around a throat dry as sandpaper "—am a shifter."

Her expressive features ran the gamut. He couldn't decipher her emotional state because her face changed so quickly. She said something in Irish just before she unsnapped her seat harness and launched herself at him with tears coursing down her cheeks.

Damn it!

He sprang to his feet and pushed her back into her seat, holding her there easily, while muttering in German and cursing fate, the gods, anyone who might be listening.

"Tut mir so leid, dies zu tun Fräulein." Lars drew back a fist, prepared to deliver a blow to render her unconscious.

She spoke to him in Irish, and then switched to English between sobs. "*Stad.* Stop. I doona know what you're saying. I doona speak German. Why would you be hitting me? Sure and I'm a shifter too."

CHAPTER 9

$\mathcal{H}$e froze, not certain he'd heard right. "What? What did you just say?"

She wriggled against his hand splayed across her chest. "Let go of me. I'm a shifter, same as you. I wanted to hug you, and you tossed me back into my seat like I was a rag mop dolly." Tamara tapped at a single ebony claw extruding from the tip of his index finger. Lars fought a sheepish grin, but it was a losing battle. He sank back into his seat with stern exhortations to his cat to retreat.

He wanted to draw her into his arms, hold her close, but he felt suddenly shy. Just because they shared the same magic—and made each other hotter than hell—it didn't necessarily mean a thing, other than he could let his guard down a few notches. "Did I hurt you?"

"No. I was more startled than hurt." She rubbed at the reddened place on her upper chest where he'd held her and shot him a rueful grin. "Either I'll be learning German, or you'll be brushing up on your Irish."

He snorted. "Gaelic, Irish, and Welsh are probably the only languages where I cannot hold my own."

"That's often the way of it. German is almost the only European language I don't know." She folded her fingers together and rested her chin on them. "Sure and you're a mountain cat. I recognized the claw."

"What are you?" Curiosity burned deep. He wanted to see her in her other form, wanted to get to know all of her.

"The same."

Joy burned a path through his soul. What were the odds? To hell with caution. He started to open his arms, invite her into his lap, when the plane beeped a warning. Lars turned his attention to the instruments, made a minor course correction, and got up to shut the cockpit door, which was what had spurred the alarm. Overwhelmed by her revelation, he wanted to pull her against him and never let go. Instead, he forced himself to take a few steps back. It was wonderful, stupendous, amazing they shared the same magic, but he still knew next to nothing about her.

He settled for brushing the top of her head with his lips before he returned to his seat and buckled in. He motioned for her to do the same. "Maybe now you can finish telling me about your life. You left off when your family moved to Dublin."

"So I did." She smiled broadly. "Well then, three of us were still in school, so it kept us busy. The older three stayed in Drogheda, at least for a while. None of them are there now. Mum developed quite a reputation as a virtuoso. Da's jewelry business flourished, but no matter how well things went, our life always felt tentative. Like a house of cards that could collapse at any moment if our secret became known."

Lars nodded sympathetically. He understood exactly what she meant. It was one of many reasons he'd remained a confirmed loner. He gestured for her to keep talking. She had a wonderful voice. Low and lyrical, it was like a balm with her Irish brogue softening the consonants and blurring the vowels.

"Not much more to tell. Not really. I went to University College in Dublin, graduated with a degree in journalism, and went to work for the *Irish Times*. I've traveled much of the world writing stories and taking pictures."

"Boyfriends?" Lars gripped the edges of his seat. It was a hard question, but he wanted to know.

Tamara shook her head. "Oh, and I've had my share, but none of them stuck. See, I had this huge secret." She winked. "There was no easy way to find men who wouldn't be blowing my cover. I was engaged once, ten years ago when I was but nineteen."

"What happened?"

She shrugged. "What always happens when you're too young to be in love? Mum warned me he wasn't like us. I'm still not quite sure how she knew, but she did. Once the first blush of sex wore off, we tired of one another and went our separate ways." She quirked an inquisitive brow. "Your turn."

Lars just stared at her. Her request was reasonable. Why was he so unprepared for it?

She laughed, a rich, pleasing sound. "Sure and you look as if you just swallowed an elephant."

An image of her statement formed in his mind, and he laughed too. "I did not think beyond finding out about you. Of course you would want to know more about me."

Shining blue eyes augured into him. She nodded. "Now that I know what you are, I sense you're one of the old ones. My parents are old like that. Me and the current batch of sibs are something like their third or fourth family."

He grinned. "They must like making babies."

She drew her brows into a thoughtful line. "That too, but I'm thinking more of it is they're worried our race will die out."

He tipped his head her way. "Good thing some of us are on top of that. I certainly have not produced so much as a single offspring."

"Tell me," she said. "Everything."

Where to begin? Lars picked through the shards of his life and understood he could hit the high points with very little effort. "I have always been what you might call a mercenary—a soldier for hire. The lifestyle appealed to me. Once upon a time, we were warriors, well-loved, revered. Not so much in modern life."

He took a breath and scanned the instruments to buy himself a moment to think. "You are correct about me being one of the elders, yet I am younger than many. I was born in 1646 and came to the U.S. around the time of the Revolutionary War. I have faded in and out of lives, so no one would notice I did not age as they did. I have known Garen—and a few others—for much of my life. We have always worked together.

"I should not tell you this. Not yet, anyway, but Rubicon International is all those like us. It is one reason you would fit."

"But I'm far from a warrior." She gazed at her lap and then looked at him. "The bald truth of it is what I did to Jaret sickened me."

He nodded. "All that means is you have a conscience. You did not back out or run shrieking from your rooms. You finished what you began. It is the same for us all. When you meet Miranda, perhaps she will tell you about one of her last assignments in a brothel for human slaves. She almost lost everything freeing them."

"She must be very brave."

"Courage comes from the heart." He tapped his breastbone. "You have a big heart."

Tamara shook her head. "Not so big. I was scared. So scared I dithered back and forth. Weeks passed when I could have...done something." She sucked in a shaky breath. "There were nights I'd circle the bed with my knife in my hand. I'd get the blade close to him, but damn me if I could force myself forward. I'd creep back to the living room and stuff a towel in my mouth, so he wouldn't hear me crying."

"What made the difference?" Lars thought he knew, but it would be good for her to verbalize it, so it sank in.

She pursed her lips until they flattened into a hard line. When she spoke, her voice vibrated with outrage. "I was sick of him." She patted her chin with the back of one hand. "Sure and I'd had it up to here with Jaret Chen. Every other night he was stoned, so I could get out of sex because he was more interested in his dope and just fell asleep. That night, he put off his shot..." She gulped air. "I, he..." Her voice trailed off, and her face splotched with shame.

"I will not judge you, *liebchen*."

She twisted her mouth into a disgusted moue. "I'd already decided back at the casino that I was going to...finish things, but after we got to our rooms, he made me touch myself. He's a voyeur, one of them that likes to watch. I started out making a game of it, but I made myself come—twice." She swallowed hard, but didn't drop her gaze. "I was afraid if I stayed with him much longer, I'd be drawn into his sickness, his craziness. If that happened, I'd have been lost. Even as things were, he'd never have let me walk away. I knew too much. Eventually, I'd have ended up dead, just like poor Moira."

Tamara inhaled raggedly. "He somehow discovered what Moira was and killed her because she was a shifter. I didn't find that out until he was dying and he called me an abomination. He knew in those last moments I was her sister."

"Did you shift?"

She nodded mutely. "My cat forced her way out once he came after me and threw me on the floor. He was choking the very life out of me, and my cat refused to let us die."

Lars reached across the few inches separating their seats and took her hand. "Thank you for trusting me."

Her nostrils flared. "Sure and that was harder than telling you about my magic."

"Because your magic is something you were born with and cannot change. Your actions with Jaret were a choice, one that embarrasses you. I have done many things I am not proud of. We make choices in the field, often when we cannot think as clearly as we would like."

Tamara gripped his hand. "What you said helps. Maybe I can forgive myself, but not quite yet. How much longer until we land?"

"A bit less than two hours." He pointed at her mineral water.

She plucked it from the drink holder built into her seat and handed it to him. "I'll find us another. Back in a moment." She got to her feet, moved to his side, and brushed her lips over his. "It will take a wee bit of time for all this to sink in."

"You have lived through a lot in a few short hours. Be gentle with yourself."

She cupped his face between her hands. "I'm still annoyed I spent even one extra minute with Jaret, let alone weeks. By all the blessed saints, I waited until I was nearly lost." She closed her eyes and pressed her lips together, shaking her head back and forth.

"Hush." He wrapped an arm around her and held onto her neck for a long moment. "You have time, *liebchen*. All the time you need to come to terms with what you did."

She straightened. "Thank you." Her footsteps faded as she left the cockpit.

He hoped what he'd said was true. Lars had a feeling at least one pitched battle stood between her and the time he'd promised. Jaret's operation spanned the globe, and they didn't seem to be taking the loss of one of their key players lying down.

TAMARA WANTED to skip down the plane's aisle. She'd kept a watchful eye on Lars, and he hadn't even flinched when she'd revealed her appalling behavior with Jaret. Maybe there was hope he could care for her. She was just balancing two bottles of mineral water, a box of crackers, and some sliced cheese when the plane lurched to one side and the ride got bumpy. They must've hit an air pocket. To compensate, she spread her feet in a wider stance and bent to troll through another cupboard.

"Return to the cockpit now!" Lars' voice crackled through the headset she'd never removed.

Her heart slammed into her throat. Not an air pocket. Something must be wrong with the plane. She hurtled down the aisle. The cockpit door was shut. Her hands were full, so she kicked it.

Lars pulled it inward, his face a study in determination. "Into your seat. Now. Fasten your harness. It will get very rough."

Food and water fell from her nerveless fingers and tumbled to the floor as she scrambled to obey. "What's wrong?"

He dove into his own seat and buckled in. "We have lost an engine, although I do not understand how it happened. The instruments did not note a malfunction. The right engine quit with no warning. We might have sucked something into it, but generally birds do not fly this high."

Her stomach twisted into a burning knot. She clenched her hands together in her lap to stop them from shaking. "Are we going to crash?"

He looked away from his instruments long enough to flash her a thumbs-up sign. "Not on my watch. I do not have time to explain fully, but left rudder will cancel much of the yaw from the dead right engine. Still, our landing will be difficult."

Questions blasted through her mind, but Tamara ignored them. She didn't want to disturb his concentration by asking for reassurances beyond what he'd already given her. Lars held several conversations over the radio. She picked up that they'd declared an emergency and would be landing at the nearest airport, which was Casper, Wyoming. Despite dire straits, Lars was cool and collected. Her admiration for him grew by leaps and bounds as she watched him maintain their course, his hands and feet coaxing the disabled plane through the air. He knew exactly what to do and acted as if things like this were second nature.

In short order, they were lined up with the runway, dropping lower and lower. Fire trucks stood along both sides, their bright red color easily visible. "Brace yourself," Lars said. The plane hit, bounced, and hit again. Three bounces later, they catapulted down the runway.

"Fuck!" he sputtered. "Goddammit. No brakes."

The plane skidded from side to side as Lars jammed the rudders sequentially. Finally, the plane slowed and rolled to a stop. Emergency personnel converged on the plane, spraying it with some sort of foam.

Tamara blew out a tense, shaky breath. "We had two separate problems?"

He nodded, his expression grim as death. "Someone tampered with the brakes—and altered both their gauge and warning lights. We would not have found out until it was too late. Apparently, there was just enough pressure left in the lines to allow us to taxi to our takeoff point without alerting me something was amiss." He shut his eyes for a long moment. "Our engine failure was a godsend in disguise. If we had been one of many planes in a pattern coming in to land, I would not have been able to stop, and we would probably have plowed into another plane once we were on the ground. At least here, they cleared the runway for us."

The enormity of what he said bit deep. She clawed at her throat to get more air—except it didn't work very well. "Chen's men," she croaked.

"Who else?" Lars growled. "Keep quiet, *fraulein*. About everything."

The radio crackled to life. Lars spoke into it, explaining the brake failure and saying they'd open the plane's door immediately. He stood and extended a hand to her. "We will go into the terminal and rent a car." He removed his headset and switched it off. She raised an eyebrow.

He nodded, so she mimicked his actions and tossed her headset atop his. Once no one could hear them, he bent close to her ear. "Now would be an excellent time to amp up that brogue. They will question us. Follow my lead. I do not see how they can detain us, but it may take time before they let us go. That this is a rental aircraft will not help our situation."

"Should I masquerade as your copilot?"

"No. They will have ample time to check your credentials, and they would sniff out a lie."

She started to say they may as well remain within the confines of the Casper airport because there was nowhere to run where Chen's people couldn't find them, but it sounded so defeatist, she held her peace. Lars was brave and confident. Maybe if she paid close attention, some of it might rub off on her.

He placed a hand under her elbow and propelled her out of the cockpit. Twisting, he slung the straps to his bags over one shoulder and picked up her suitcase. The rear door chose to be stubborn. As soon as Lars coaxed it open with a combination of German curses and a few stout kicks, they followed two uniformed guards across the tarmac.

An hour later, they were still in a small office answering questions. The guards had examined both their passports, culled through their luggage, and questioned Lars closely about his revolver. Thank God, he'd had it stowed in his luggage and not in an ankle holster.

Both guards were middle-aged, with muscular bodies and short-cropped brownish hair shading to gray. Hard, flat blue eyes stared at Tamara. "Indulge me, Ms. MacBride. You met this man—" he hooked a thumb at Lars "—at the Nice airport. You'd never seen him before in your life, and you got into a private plane with him?"

"Sure and that's about the size of it. I dinna have aught better to do. He's a fine looking man, wouldn't ye say?" She winked lewdly. "I could do far worse."

The other guard's phone rang. He barked a *yes*, listened for a moment, and beckoned to his cohort before stepping outside the interrogation room. Tamara glanced at Lars, but he shook his head. Who knew? Maybe the room was bugged. She resettled herself in a straight-backed chair, but no matter which way she sat, it wasn't comfortable.

The door swung open. "Get up," the first guard snapped. "You're free to go."

Lars stood, smiled, and extended a hand. Neither guard reached for it. "As you will, gentlemen." He dropped his hand to his side. "Could you recommend a decent A&P to repair my airplane, so I might see it returned to Ermstatter in Nice?"

"That's been handled. Someone from your firm, a Garen LeRochefort, stepped up to the plate on your behalf."

"Excellent." Lars placed his hand on Tamara's shoulder. "My dear, it appears we are free to locate other transportation."

"You won't be flying anything like that Gulfstream without a copilot," one of the guards snarled. "They may be looser about regulations in Europe, but the FAA—"

"I would not dream of it," Lars cut in pointedly. He picked up his bags, along with hers, and motioned for her to follow him.

She got to her feet and opened her mouth, intent on figuring out what they were going to do, but he murmured, "Not now. You would be surprised which walls have ears."

It was good advice. It also drove home how woefully ignorant she was of the spy trade. She'd been damned lucky to have gotten in and out that mess with Jaret.

Sure and I almost didn't escape, she reminded herself.

Lars stopped at a bank kiosk and inserted a credit card. The machine spit a stack of U.S. money into his hand. She rummaged in her purse and pulled out her wallet, meaning to get some funds of her own, but he took it from her hand and placed it back into her handbag.

What the hell? I can't talk. I can't use the money kiosk...

Even though she respected Lars' instincts, Tamara gritted her teeth together. Would she be reduced to little more than a helpless child before everything was said and done? To mask her annoyance, she picked a neutral topic as they stood in line at the car rental counter. "You were wonderfully competent after we lost that engine. You knew just what to do. It was as if things like that happen to you every day."

"Thank Christ they do not. It is why I practice, though. Garen flies too. He and I simulate emergencies, and we work our way through them." As if on cue, Lars' phone jangled. He pulled it out, tapped the display, and said, "*Ja?*"

The conversation was short and one-sided. Less than a minute passed before Lars disconnected and pocketed his phone. Tamara wanted to ask about it, and about why he hadn't let her use her own credit card at the bank kiosk, but they'd finally moved to the head of the queue.

"How can I help you, sir?" The car rental representative smiled blandly. Though young, she appeared tired. Blonde hair hung untidily about her face, and her uniform shirt had come untucked.

"We would like a one-way rental. Four wheel drive, please."

"Very good, sir. Where will you be leaving our car?"

"Jackson Hole, Wyoming."

CHAPTER 10

Tamara kept her mouth shut until they were in a full-sized SUV, following directions from its dashboard navigation system. She peered at the map on the car's navigational display and zoomed out so she could get some perspective. "It's a long way," she ventured. "Two hundred seventy-five miles. Let's see, that would be just over four hundred kilometers."

Lars reached across the console and grasped her hand. "We will be driving through some of the most beautiful country in the world. Unfortunately, it is growing dark. Our journey will not take long. Maybe five hours. We are meeting Garen tomorrow at noon at the Jackson Hole airport."

"Sure and I wondered why we were going to a ski resort."

"Depending on what you'd like to do, I had thought we could stop for the night in Riverton. That is just over a hundred sixty kilometers." He glanced fondly at her, his strong-boned face illuminated by the dash lights. "That way, the most stunning part of our drive will occur in daylight."

"And we'll have a few hours to ourselves." She squeezed his hand. The idea of spending the night with the man beside her thrilled her beyond words.

"Yes, if you wish it."

A formality sat beneath his words, as if he didn't want her to think he was taking anything for granted. Disappointment pricked. She wanted him to…to what? Bleed enthusiasm? Somehow, she suspected it wasn't his style.

She leaned back against the well-padded leather seat, inhaling its rich scent. "I can't think of anything I'd rather do." She raised his hand to her lips, kissed the back of it, and took a chance. "Or anyone I'd rather be with."

Breath whistled from between his teeth. "You will have to be patient with me. I know little of wooing a woman."

She snorted. "Not that I'm any great expert in the wooing department. I'm guessing we can help each other."

He pulled into a well-lighted shopping center. "I like the sound of that. While it would be charming to talk of love and courtship, I fear we must discuss less pleasant things." He paused for a beat. "Garen will have alternative identification for us. That will not help us tonight. Whoever is after us has figured out we are together."

"Is that why you wouldn't let me use the money changing machine?"

"*Ja.* It is bad enough I have been leaving a trail a mile wide, but I cannot help that. I had planned on flying from Nice back to Germany in a twin engine prop plane I left at the airport."

Tamara considered the implications. "Is Lars your real name?"

"One of them."

"What would you like me to call you?"

He caressed her thigh. "Does it really matter? I am who I am, regardless of labels."

She thought about it. "So long as I can call you something and you'll be answering, that's probably good enough." She glanced at brilliant neon signs. "Why did we stop here?"

"We need a few things. If we wait until we get to Riverton, all the stores will be closed." Lars got out of the car, walked around to her side, and held her door open for her. He offered his hand and she took it, just before she wrapped her arms around him and laid her head on his shoulder. He pulled her against him. The heat of him seared her, even through her clothes. He tilted his head and kissed her, his lips barely brushing hers before he stepped away and closed her car door. Once he'd hit the clicker to activate the door locks, he took her hand again and leaned close. "I would like nothing better than to hold you in my arms for hours, explore your body, but we must move quickly. Once we purchase a few items, we shall put distance between us and Casper, Wyoming."

She matched her whisper to his. "Do *they* know we're here?"

He shrugged as they walked toward a high rounded arch blazoned with SPORTS AUTHORITY. "It is possible they do not since our flight plan lists Boeing Field as our destination. After another hour, they will know we did not land there. If they are monitoring an aviation band transceiver, they already know what has happened." He gestured for her to precede him into the store.

"Do you believe they're responsible for the engine malfunction too?" Her heart beat a tattoo against her ribs as fear threatened to take over.

Lars drew his brows together in thought. "It would make sense. If that is the case, then they would certainly know the plane went down within a certain area, though not precisely which airport I choose."

Before she went inside, Tamara turned and raked the semi-dark parking lot, hunting for anything suspicious. Her anxiety was back in spades. If Chen's men knew where they were, they needed to get moving straightaway. "What are we buying?"

"Warmer clothing for you. Sleeping bags in case we have another unexplained engine failure on the mountain roads between here and our destination. Maybe a shotgun, but I doubt they will sell me one with my German passport and international driver's license." He made a grab for a cart and they worked their way through the store. Because she settled for holding clothing up to her and didn't try anything on, they were at the checkout stand in less than half an hour. He'd been right about being unable to buy a shotgun.

She snugged a green, fluffy coat around herself as soon as the checker scanned its tag, grateful for its protection and followed it with a black knitted hat and leather gloves. Monte Carlo had been warm. The temperature here must be somewhere in the minus rating. Quite aside from the ambient temperature, she felt chilled to her core, certain a band of thugs would jump them at any moment.

I've got to get hold of myself. Lars doesn't seem scared.

"Thanks for the clothing. Sure and I wasn't aware how ice-cold I was, probably because we spent all that time in the airport. How cold is it here?" she asked as they made their way back to their rental SUV.

He glanced at his watch and tapped a few buttons. "Minus seven centigrade, which is about twenty Fahrenheit."

"Brrrr. It never gets this cold in Ireland. Well, hardly ever."

"It is early March." He popped the hatch and tossed their packages inside.

She gave him a long hug before getting back into the car, reluctant to let go. Even better, he seemed as reluctant as she. Where their bodies fit together, she felt the unmistakable bulge of his erection, heard his breath quicken, and felt need in the fingers he wound around her head, cradling it.

"Good thing we got those sleeping bags," she murmured against his shoulder. "We could be laying them out in the back and—"

He laughed and helped her into the car. "That might be the most attractive offer I have ever had." She laid a hand over the belled-out front of his trousers, and he pressed into her. "You are not making this easy, *liebchen*."

"Maybe I'm not trying to."

"Imp." He closed her door, got in on his side, and ferried the car back onto an expressway. They left Casper behind quickly. Time passed, maybe an hour. Lights thinned and then died out almost entirely. As if he divined her thoughts, he said, "We are passing large ranches. This is cattle country, but they grow hay and wheat here as well."

She grinned. "I wasn't needing an agricultural lesson. I was looking for a secluded spot we could pull off the road."

He groaned.

She suspected his erection hadn't subsided one whit. Her nipples pebbled, and she pressed her thighs together. Even if they only had a quickie, it would take the edge off her hunger for him. She straddled the console separating them. He shoved a hand between her legs and she writhed against his fingers as they drummed a sensuous rhythm atop her vulva. She pressed her hand over his, showing him what she needed until a climax ripped through her. Once it subsided, she slid back into her seat and reached for him, but he captured her hand.

"Wait. An exit is just ahead."

He ferried the car off the expressway, down a frontage road, and into a thick grove of aspen trees, before he killed the engine. "This is risky," he panted, "but so is life. Slide your pants off."

With a bit of awkward maneuvering, he ended up in her seat with her kneeling over his lap. She'd been right about him still being hard. He sank his cock into her body and gripped her ass cheeks with both hands. She closed her mouth over his, delighting in their kiss and the feel of his hard, insistent lips against hers. Lars plumbed her with his tongue and his cock. She squirmed against him, jamming her clit against his pubic bone. Another peak began low in her belly. His cock swelled even bigger inside her. She tightened her muscles around him and felt release zing through her, setting every nerve ending on fire. Moments later, his cock pulsated and semen gushed into her. He tightened his grip on her ass and made an amazing purring sound, exactly like a big cat that had just claimed his mate.

They held one another for long moments while they caught their breath before disentangling limbs and body parts. "Sure and maybe someday we'll get to do that in a bed like proper lovers," she teased.

"By then we will be so used to odd nooks and crannies, we may need them to heat our blood."

"Speak for yourself." She blotted her pussy with tissues from the glove box. "I'll take as much of that—" she patted his still half-hard cock "—as I can get. Wherever, whenever."

He kissed her, slowly, tenderly, and then returned to the driver's seat. Kilometers passed in a companionable silence. She dozed in fits and starts, satiated from having had him inside her. The sound of his voice called her back.

"Much as I hate to wake you—" he stroked her cheek with calloused fingertips "—we must speak further about unpleasant things. By now, Chen's men must surely know we did not land in Seattle. It will not take much sophistication in the way of intelligence to discover where we did land, if they did not know already. We need a hotel that takes cash and does not put our identification on file. What that often means is a lower class establishment." He set the car's cruise control and reached for a bottle of water in the console between them. She unscrewed the lid and handed it over.

Tamara glanced behind them. The back seat was huge, and it looked as if it folded down. "I have an idea. Why not just spread out those sleeping bags. Then we could get some supper and sleep in the back of the car if we can't find a hotel."

"You would be willing to do that?" He stared at her until the car swerved, and he was forced to return his attention to the road.

"I suggested it, didn't I? We did a spot of camping when I was growing up. I didn't like getting wet, so when it rained, I'd always make a dash for the car—before anyone could beat me to it."

He chuckled. "It rains a lot in the United Kingdom."

"It certainly does. It got so Mum just laid my bag out in the car. Said it saved her the effort of moving things around and getting even wetter than she would have if she just stayed in our big, canvas tent."

"Thank you for your offer." Lars' formal tone was back. "It means a lot that you would offer to be uncomfortable just to…" His words faded.

"Sure and I'd do damn near anything to hold you in my arms all night. Are you kidding? It would be fun. An adventure." She bounced a bit in her seat.

"Good you did not lose your taste for adventures in Monte Carlo."

Something about the deadpan undertone in his words brought her up short. "Isn't that the truth. I know this isn't a game. Do you suppose they're out there somewhere—" she gestured toward her side window "—following us?"

"It is what I would do in their place." His words were solemn. "It is also why, no matter where we wait out the night, one of us must have all their faculties about them at all times. Because you lack training, I will watch over you."

Something sweet and poignant in his words shook her to her soul. "You're taking care of me."

"*Ja.* I have been taking care of you ever since your taxi jumped the curb."

So he has.

"I didn't understand then how much I needed your help."

"And now you do?" His wry humor warmed her.

"Probably not as thoroughly as you understand it, no, but sure and I'm getting there."

"We can teach each other, *liebchen.*"

"I like it when you call me that. There are Gaelic endearments, too, like *mo croi.*"

"It does not matter what we call one another." He raised his hand from her lap and tapped her breastbone before tapping his own. "When one heart calls to another, there is little need for language."

"That's beautiful."

"No, *liebchen*. You are beauty. Your eyes remind me of a restless sea. Your hair is like a shining crown, and your lips are full, kissable, perfect."

"Stop." She stifled a pleased giggle. "I'll become insufferable. For a gent who was clueless about how to court a woman, I'd say you're doing a fairly decent job."

"My cat wants to meet yours."

"What?" She started, astounded by what he'd said, by the rapid shift of topics.

"Did your parents teach you nothing about shifter matings?"

Defensiveness sparred with embarrassment. "It wasn't Mum's fault. She tried, but I'd never listen."

"Why not?"

"I didn't figure I'd ever meet up with another one like me, much less fall in love—" She clapped a hand over her mouth. "Whoops."

"What is between us feels like the beginnings of love. It is why our animal sides must meet."

"See and there's another reason for us pulling the car off into the woods and sleeping in the back of it. We could, um, shift and run about for a bit." Tamara forced herself to stop talking. She was babbling because she felt nervous. Outside her immediate family, she'd never shown anyone her animal side—until the night she killed Jaret.

"You do not have to do anything that makes you ill at ease." Lars' deep voice rumbled comfortably across the space between them. "My other form comes in handy in my work."

"So much time goes by between when I shift, I sometimes forget about that side of myself."

"I surmised as much." He hesitated. "I am certain your cat is just as beautiful as you are."

Her face heated. She glanced at the nav system and noticed they were only twenty miles from Riverton. A quick conversion told her it was thirty-two kilometers because she still had a hard time thinking in miles.

"Did your Mum tell you anything about shifter pairings?" he pressed.

"You've asked twice," she said, thinking what it might mean. "I'm guessing there is something important you want to make certain I know."

"You are astute. Bright as well as beautiful."

Tamara rolled her eyes. "Just tell me." She watched his profile, illuminated by muted light from the car's dashboard.

"Though I did not mean for us to make love like a couple of randy teenagers in the car, it happened. So we must be careful."

"Why? I can't get pregnant unless I will it."

He shook his head. "No. Not that. And shifters are immune from human diseases, so that is not it, either. Once we shift—and we will—we cannot make love in our animal forms unless we are certain we want to spend our lives together."

Her ears perked up. This was the first time she'd heard anything like that. "Why?"

A muscle in his jaw worked. "When I meet your parents, I will inquire why they did not do a better job educating their offspring. Shifters mate for life. Making love in shifted form cements the bond and will make it impossible for you to love anyone but me, whether we remain together or go our separate ways. It works the same for me."

Motivated by his seriousness, she dropped her bantering tone. "Och, I see. Mum tried to talk with me about the mate bond, but I wasn't having any of it. Is any of this written down?"

"*Ja*. And carefully guarded. Are none of your brothers married to shifters?"

"None of them ever married." She culled through her memory, recalling shrouded conversations between her parents and other shifters. "Things got so bad for us in Ireland, we hid what we were. If anyone trolled for a mate, they were damned quiet about it."

He pounded a fist on the steering wheel. "It is why I chose to spend my time among shifters. Humans are afraid of their own shadows, but they have done a hell of a job intimidating us by slapping rules atop other rules. What I have never understood is why we did not mobilize, fight back."

"That's an easy one." She blew out an exasperated breath. "When you're taught to be invisible, sure and it's a hard habit to break."

CHAPTER 11

*L*ars took them to a charming log building for dinner where they shared rare steaks, crisp greens, and bread fresh from the oven, along with a bottle of excellent Cabernet. They were on their third motel, had just pulled into the parking lot, when Tamara laid a hand on his arm. "Let's just find somewhere out of town and sleep in the woods. It's late, nearly the middle of the night. We won't be there so long as to arouse suspicion."

"If you are certain." He felt protective of her and didn't want her to be cold, or to want for anything. He'd begun to resurrect the conversation about shifter matings and mate bonds over dinner, but the restaurant had been too crowded for such a sensitive topic.

"I'm certain. The last two inns refused cash without running your identification. Like as not, so will this one. I'd rather be out of doors than in some of the down-at-the-heels places we went past."

He leaned toward her, inhaling her unique scent. Privately, he'd been convinced after the first motel that none of them would accept anonymous guests, no matter how empty their parking lot was. Lars nosed the big car west, heading toward Jackson on Highway 26. Though he hadn't spent much time in this part of the United States, he recalled convoluted country, filled with buttes and mesas, both to the north and south of them.

Thank Christ the car had a huge gas tank. He hadn't been forced to use plastic since hitting the ATM machine at the Casper airport. It would've been a piece of cake for Chen's men to trace their emergency landing in Casper, and easy for them to discover Lars had rented a car. What would be more difficult would be deciding which way out of Casper to deploy manpower hunting for them— unless someone either bribed or threatened the car rental agency to reveal their destination.

Sixty-five kilometers clicked by. He'd spent enough time in the States, he made the transition from miles to kilometers seamlessly. When he figured they were about as deep in mesa country as they were likely to get, he hunted for a promising side road. No point in getting too far off the highway. He glanced at Tamara. She was dozing again. *Good.* She needed rest.

Running on instincts that had rarely failed him, Lars flipped the car into four wheel drive and guided it along faint, sandy roads until he was satisfied they were as hidden as they were likely to get without a whole lot more effort. Small ice and snow patches butted up against stark rock formations. He turned off the engine. Silence, so thick it was almost palpable, rose around them.

"Are we there?" she asked sleepily.

He reached over to ruffle her hair, but she still wore the knitted cap he'd insisted she buy. "*Ja, liebchen.*"

She cocked her head to one side, leaning into his hand. "It's quiet. Sure and I don't even hear any animals."

"There is much empty land in the United States. It is very different from Europe and the United Kingdom in that respect."

"I was thinking—" she began.

"And here I thought you were asleep." His chest swelled with caring for the woman next to him.

"Well, that too," she admitted. "Now that we're here, I'll be taking you up on your offer."

Lars felt confused. "What offer, *fraulein*?"

"Och, and I like *liebchen*—beloved—better. The offer to let our cats meet."

He sucked in a breath. She'd been so gun shy, he'd assumed that part of things wouldn't happen for quite some time.

She must've mistaken his hesitation because she added, "Isn't it safe here?"

"Safe enough. At least I believe it to be. You took me by surprise. Give me a moment or two outside, and I will let you know." He got out of the car and inhaled deeply. The frigid night air seared his lungs, but it was fresh and dry and smelled of the desert. Of little rodents, cactus, and sagebrush. He dialed in his cat senses and did it again. Nothing human lived anywhere close. Beyond the distant thrum of cars on the highway, he didn't hear or smell anything that might indicate someone was tracking them.

He walked to her side of the car and opened the door. She scrambled out, ignoring his extended hand. He felt her draw magic, concentrate it, and lunged for her arm. "Take your clothes off first, otherwise they will be ruined."

She looked sheepish, and then began to laugh. Tension bled out of the moment. "If I hadn't already told you how infrequently I do this, I'd surely have given myself away. It's lucky I remembered when we were back at the airport terminal before I healed myself."

He moved next to her, tugged the hat from her head and the gloves from her hands. She bent, untied her shoes, toed them off, and tossed them into the car along with her socks and the rest of her clothes as she removed them.

He watched her body emerge, mesmerized. Though he'd seen parts of her, he'd never seen her totally nude. The perfection of her sleekly muscled form stole his breath.

She wrapped her arms around herself. "Aren't you going to join me?" she asked through chattering teeth.

He sought words to tell her how striking she was, how incredible, but English eluded him. All he could come up with was

German. He swallowed hard. "I will lock the car with your things in it. The keys will be in front of the left rear wheel."

"What about your clothes?"

"If something untoward happens, they will be the least of my problems." He began to strip, starting with his shoes. "Go ahead and find your cat form." He grinned. "She will keep you warm."

The air around her shimmered. A knockout of a mountain cat emerged with a thick, tawny pelt, and Tamara's beautiful, blue eyes. The cat grinned at him, licked her chops, and purred long and low. His cat raged for release. Lars forgot about folding his clothes. He stuffed them beneath the car, along with the keys, and opened the pathway to free his cat.

"You're silver," she murmured. *"Just like your eyes."*

He rubbed his flank against her and licked her snout. She nuzzled him back. His cat cock hardened. To quell the sexual heat flaring painfully in his loins, he suggested, *"Shall we run?"*

Tamara made a noise between a purr and a snarl. *"Sure and I'd rather make love, but running is good too."*

"Remember what I told you about joining in this form." Hope speared him. He wanted nothing more than to be bound to Tamara, but he understood the need for caution. Now that he saw her as a cat, he felt the mate bond and was even more certain she was his chosen one, but they had to have at least a small space of time when they weren't running for their lives to make a decision that would bind them forever.

She leapt into the air and took off at a dead run. He charged after her. They chased one another, nipping, rolling, playing, until both were breathless. His sense of time was diminished in this form, but he was certain over an hour passed. Without exchanging words, they loped back to the car and called their human forms. He shook sand out of his clothes before getting back into them and opened the car so she could dress.

By the time she was covered, he'd folded down the back seat and laid out the sleeping bags. It wouldn't be the most comfortable bed since he hadn't thought to buy air mattresses, but it wasn't all that long before dawn. He wanted to be at the airport in plenty of time, and it was still a couple hours' driving time. Plus, they'd want to stop for coffee and breakfast.

He tucked her into the nest he'd made when he'd unzipped the bags and laid one atop the other, got in the other side, and hit the clicker to lock the car. When he held out his arms, she snuggled against him. Tenderness flooded him as he wrapped his arms around her. "I was right. Your cat is just as gorgeous as you are."

"Not that I've seen that many shifters in shifted form, but sure and I've never seen a silver cat before. You're amazing." She quieted, but he sensed she wanted to say more.

"What?" he prodded. "We should have no secrets between us."

She propped herself on an elbow and gazed at him, her heart in her eyes. "I had no idea it could be like that. I've never shifted just to play, and it felt incredible, like I was born to be her." She took a measured breath and went on. "My cat is happy too. I don't ever remember sensing her emotions before, but her joy is so deep and so poignant, it's as if she's dancing inside me."

He felt the smile begin in his heart before it found its way to his lips. "It is the same with me. I have always embraced my dual nature, but my cat has never been so exultant. We have been waiting for you all our lives."

Tears formed in her eyes, making them glow. "My mum, she tried to tell me I shouldn't settle for less than a shifter mate. I told her sure and wishful thinking it was, since the odds of meeting another of us was so remote." A single tear tracked down one cheek.

He pulled her into his arms again. "The past does not matter, *liebchen*. Only the future. Our future." He covered her mouth with his. Lars didn't plan to make love with her, but his cock was still hard from when he'd been in cat form. Even beyond his physical need, Lars craved the woman in his arms with his soul.

She opened her mouth beneath his and curved her arms around his body, holding him tight against her. Unlike earlier, Lars didn't hurry. He kissed her until the body in his arms melted against him, and she made delightful mewling noises deep in her throat. When he raised his mouth from hers and strung kisses down the side of her face to the hollow in her neck, she murmured, "We could have saved a wee bit of time by not getting dressed."

"I did not plan this." He nuzzled her neck. "You are nigh onto irresistible."

"You'll be turning this poor girl's head with all that fancy talk." She slipped a hand between their bodies and curled her fingers around his erection, still covered by his trousers. His breath quickened. In the small corner of his mind that wasn't swamped with lust, he didn't understand why he couldn't keep his hands off her. It hadn't been that long since they'd sated themselves.

He tugged her top up to expose her breasts. Moonlight spilled into the car, lending her skin a silvery glow. Her nipples were already puckered. He bent and kissed first one, and then the other. She arched her back, wove her fingers into his hair, and murmured in Irish. Her hips thrust rhythmically as he suckled her, and he sensed her increasing arousal. It stoked his own until he trembled on the edge of orgasm. It was as if everything he did to her amplified itself until he felt it in his own body.

Lars drew away and gazed down at Tamara. She gazed back, her eyes glistening with need and warmth. Slowly, she reached between them, undid his pants, and drew his cock out. He felt her spread liquid heat around his exquisitely sensitive glans, and understood his own fluid had escaped. She gripped his shaft and milked it with her hand. So aroused he could barely contain himself, he laid his hand over hers. "I need to be inside you. If you keep that up, I will spend on your beautiful belly."

"Such an old-fashioned word." She helped him undo her pants and pushed them down so she could free one leg.

"Maybe I am an old-fashioned man." Lars took hold of his cock and guided it between her legs until his cockhead seated firmly against her opening. She moaned, drew her legs up, and latched them around his back. He took his time pushing into her and savored every centimeter of him surrounded by her lush heat. When he hit bottom, he stopped moving and contracted his muscles until he felt an answering twitch from hers.

He supported himself on his arms and drank in her beauty. Ever so slowly, he began to move in tiny little circles. Her hips bucked beneath him, and her head fell back on her graceful stalk of a neck. She made a grab for his hips and ground herself against his body. He felt her pussy convulse around him as she came, and he rode through her peak alongside her, feeling her ecstasy in his heart. He wanted release, but he could wait. Pleasing her was everything. He'd never felt that way before. He'd been a considerate lover, but he'd always been anxious to get up and get moving once sex was over with. The emotions cascading through him, where he wanted to shield Tamara, protect her from harm, hold her next to him forever, were something new.

Tamara made a satisfied, purring sound and clamped her muscles around him. She moved her hands off his body and cupped her breasts, twirling and teasing the nipples. Watching her touch herself was a game changer. It amped up his arousal to white heat. When she moved a hand to her mouth, licked her fingers, and placed them atop her mound, he almost forgot to breathe.

Gazing at her while she touched her nipple and her clit unraveled him. Control crumbled. He withdrew and slammed himself home, never taking his eyes from the show she put on for him. His balls tightened and snugged against his body. The deep blue of her eyes drew him in, and held him.

"Yes, my love." She met him stroke for stroke, breasts and cheeks splotched with lust. "Now. Come with me now."

As if his body danced to her command, a powerful orgasm shuddered through him as her muscles contracted and released around his shaft. English abandoned him, so he murmured to her in German, telling her he adored her, that he'd care for her forever. He came back to himself gasping and panting atop her, with her arms and legs twined around his body.

"Amazing, incredible," she crooned and stroked his back. "All that aside, learning German is at the top of my to-do list."

He started to answer her, and then froze. "Ssht." He pulled his cock from the heat of her body, collected his pants and dragged them over his still throbbing member. A moment later he reconsidered. His cat form was ideal for night work, much better than his gun. Clothes would only be an impediment.

"What is it?" She kept her voice low and gathered her own clothes.

"Hold off on those clothes. I heard a car."

"But it's the middle of the night."

"Exactly." He reached for his gun, loaded it just in case. He worked automatically, without needing eyes to see what he was doing. "Have you ever fought in your cat form?"

She shook her head, eyes round with apprehension. Lars listened intently. The car had slowed, but it was definitely closer and still moving toward them.

Damn it!

He'd left tire tracks in the sandy road. They would've been easy to follow. "Listen closely. This is what we shall do. I cannot leave you in the car. You would be a sitting duck."

CHAPTER 12

*T*amara shifted from paw to paw as she waited in a shadowed overhang about fifty human paces from the car. She could cover the distance in three or four easy leaps. Lars' plan was simple enough. They'd left the car open as a trap to draw whoever hunted them. It would allow them to determine how many men they had to deal with. If it was only two, Lars said he'd take them both, striking while they leaned inside the car. If it was more than that, they'd regroup. Fortunately, they could communicate telepathically in cat form, something she already knew. Lars had told her it was possible in their human forms as well, but there hadn't been time to go into any deeper explanations.

She sensed him waiting across from her, still as death. Cats were excellent predators because they could remain so motionless, their prey never knew what hit them. Tamara felt a growl form deep in her chest and swallowed it. Her cat was thrilled by the turn of events. Tamara wasn't so sure, but she would do whatever she had to. Lars was shaping up to be the man of her dreams, the love of her life. No way would she lose him now. She pictured him above her, making love to her, and her vulva twitched.

Not now.

She dug her claws into the dirt as a distraction. A car engine grew louder and then stilled. She tried to pinpoint its location and determined it had to be somewhere behind the SUV, but on the same dirt road Lars had taken. Car doors opened, but she didn't hear them close. Maybe two, maybe three. It was hard to tell when sounds happened at the same time.

Footsteps thudded their way.

"There are three," Lars informed her just about the time she'd come to the same conclusion.

"What do you want to do?"

"Wait until they get closer, and I can see what kind of firepower they are packing."

Of course they wouldn't come empty handed. Tamara's cat wanted to leap forward, tear their fucking throats out. What was a bullet or two? Shifters had excellent restorative magic. She kept her cat in line by reminding it Lars was calling the shots. Her cat adored Lars, so that seemed to do the trick.

The men moved cautiously forward. They sported communications devices that amplified their voices, but only for one another. She wouldn't have heard them if she'd been human. As it was, every word was crystal clear.

"You sure this is the car?"

"Yeah. Plates match what our hacker picked up off the car rental site."

A third man, with a heavy accent that sounded Russian said, "I tell you. Better we riddle car with bullets. Tell boss they fought back."

"No," the first voice said in refined British English. "These two are wanted alive. Particularly the man. We've tried to get our hands on him for years."

"Holy fucking crap. Take a gander at this," the second voice, which sounded American as all get out, muttered.

"What is it?" from the Brit.

"Big cat tracks. Fresh too," the American answered. "Are there cougars in these hills?"

"That's a stupid question," the Brit snapped, sounding surly. "There must be or you wouldn't see tracks. Humph. I wonder…" He moved toward the SUV and shone a penlight into the back. Tamara got a good look at him. He resembled many of Jaret's men. Hard body, hard eyes. He was tall and muscular, dressed in black, with greasepaint on his face and a black watch cap pulled low on his head. "Fuck. They're not here."

"Maybe we got lucky," the Russian smirked. "Cats might have gotten them."

"Not very fucking likely," the American muttered. "Man's too smart for that. I fought him in Africa. Bastard had some kind of affinity for big cats. It was spooky, I tell you. They obeyed him, danced to his tune like some fucked up Pied Piper."

"Lars…?"

"Stay put."

One minute he was near her, the next, he flew through the air and drove the Brit and the Russian to the ground. The American pulled a large caliber revolver from a hidden holster. Tamara didn't stop to think. She launched herself at his back and sank her teeth deep into the side of his neck, aiming for his carotid. Blood shot into the air before he hit the ground, and it just kept pumping. She batted his gun out of range and raked her claws down his head and neck for good measure. When he tried to strangle her, she flipped him over and clawed out his eyes. If he couldn't see, he wouldn't be a threat, even if it took him a few minutes to die.

A gun went off. She spun, her tail and whiskers twitching. The Russian lay in a spreading pool of blood, maybe dead. Didn't matter since he wasn't moving. Lars was all over the Brit who'd just fired point blank into his belly. Tamara shrieked a high, feral squeal and pounded her body into the Brit's side. He went down with a *whump,* and she clawed and bit until she was drenched in his blood.

As soon as she was sure he'd never get up again, she padded to

Lars' inert body, whining. She nosed him, licked him, and could have cried once she realized he was alive. *"Heal yourself, beloved."*

"Get me into the car and drive us out of here." His mind voice was shockingly weak.

She reached for her human form and acted fast. Lars was bleeding. A puddle had formed beneath him. She drove the car right next to him, opened the back door, and tried to lift him, but his cat weighed well over two hundred pounds. After sweating and struggling, she finally had an idea and draped one of the sleeping bags so it hung half out the door. She closed the other end in the opposite door to stabilize it.

"You have to help me." She buried her hands in his fur. "Goddammit, Lars. Sure and you can't die on me. Use your claws. Dig into the fabric. If you can help even a little, I can boost you inside."

Making a gurgling sound that made her blood run cold, Lars twisted and dug his claws deep into the sleeping bag. She got behind him and pushed. Between the two of them, his cat slithered into the backseat. She took a moment and wrapped her arms around him, breathing hard from exertion.

"Hang on, dearest. I'll be figuring something out." He licked her face. She stroked his fur, murmured in Gaelic, unable to force herself to let go.

"We must leave. More will come behind them," Lars said, his voice so faint she barely heard him. Blood bubbled from his nostrils, and her heart shattered. She slammed the back door and ran around to the driver's side pulling a sweatshirt over her head as she went. No time to worry about her naked bottom half. As an afterthought, she remembered to open the other back door and move the sleeping bag so it wouldn't flap against the car as they drove.

She'd rarely driven a left hand drive car, so it took her a moment to get her bearings. She tried to go slow, so she wouldn't jostle Lars and make things worse. Once they were back on the expressway, she tried calling for him both out loud and in her mind voice, but he didn't answer. Frantic, she fished his cell phone out of the center console and pushed the redial button. Garen didn't know her from Adam, but she bet he'd pull out all the stops to help Lars.

"Yes, Lars. What's wrong?" a sleepy sounding voice said.

"Sure and 'tisn't Lars. He's hurt. I need help."

"Whoa. Slow down." Garen's voice sharpened with a suspicious undertone. "Tell me your name."

"Tamara MacBride. Let me activate FaceTime so you can see it's me." She wanted to cry, to shriek, but she couldn't afford a meltdown. Tamara split her attention between the road and the phone, found the FaceTime button, and initiated it.

"Got it," he graveled. "You look like hell, Ms. MacBride. Report."

She forced herself to speak distinctly, so her brogue wouldn't run her words together. "Gunmen came after us. Lars took a bullet. I have him in the back of the car and I'm on the highway to Jackson, but he's not talking to me. I'm scared he's going to die. Help me. Tell me where to take him to get help."

"Is he in cat form?"

"Yes."

"Goddammit."

"Talk to me." She pounded the steering wheel. "Why is that bad?"

"Because if he was strong enough, he'd have shifted back."

"What is it?" a woman's voice asked.

"Who was that?" Tamara asked, her voice trembling.

"My wife, Miranda."

"Och. Lars was telling me of her—"

"Stop. No time for social niceties. Do you have a navigational system in the car?"

"Yes."

"Tell me as closely as you can where you are."

She did, trying to keep her voice from shaking. She wanted to stop the car, wrap her body around Lars, and will him to live for her —for them.

"All right," Garen said. "I've pinpointed your position on my computer. Drive another twenty-five miles. Pull off the road at Dubois. I'm heading for the heliport on my roof right now. I'll have a bird in the air in five minutes, and I'll be to you soon. Not more than a couple of hours, three tops."

Miranda said something in the background. Garen muttered, "Yeah, probably a better idea. Miranda thinks it would go faster if you keep driving and meet the chopper in Idaho Falls."

"I can do that. I am less likely to draw attention if the car is moving."

"Tamara. They've made you."

Something cold slipped down her spine and she shivered. "What do you mean?"

"The bad guys know what you're driving. If you were one of my agents, I'd tell you to swap cars, but you probably don't know how to hot wire one. Just be careful. Lars always carries a gun. Can you shoot?"

She nodded, realized he couldn't see her, and said, "Yes."

"Is the gun where you can get to it?"

"No."

"Okay, Tamara. Take a deep breath. Stop the car when you can. No rush. Take everything nice and easy. Clean all that blood off yourself and get the gun. Keep it loaded and ready. If anyone but a cop tries to stop you, shoot to kill—and then drive like hell."

She swallowed back nausea and clutched the steering wheel so hard it made her hands ache. Words felt beyond her.

"It's pretty quiet on your end," Garen observed. "Did you hear me?"

"Yes. I'll do it."

"Shifters are tough. Keep the faith. See you soon." The line went dead.

Tamara stared at the cell phone before setting it back in the console. She listened intently with her cat senses. Lars was still breathing. Thank all the bloody saints. If he died because of the mess he'd gotten roped into saving her, she'd never be able to forgive herself. In a few kilometers, she pulled off onto the shoulder, retrieved the gun, and positioned it in the passenger seat. Next she dipped icy water from a half-frozen stream to clean herself up, using a shirt from her suitcase as a washrag. Once she'd gotten the worst of the gore off her face and hands, she yanked on the rest of her clothes and shoes, and settled back behind the wheel.

After an incident where another car flashed its brights and honked loudly, she managed to keep her car in its proper lane. The transition to driving on the right wasn't as automatic as she would've liked.

Minutes ticked by; they turned into hours. The night had developed an eerily kaleidoscopic quality when something flashed at her. Low fuel light.

Damn it.

She glanced at the miniature map on her dashboard and punched a few buttons to find the nearest petrol station. It was thirty-two kilometers. She wondered if she'd make it and slowed the car to extend its range.

The fuel gauge read below empty when she finally saw the neon display of a huge petrol station that obviously catered to truckers. Tamara pulled the car into a shadowed glade, crept into the back, and tugged a sleeping bag over Lars. She kissed his furred face, but he didn't stir.

"We're stopping for petrol," she whispered into his ear. "Not that you'd be fussing, but you must remain hidden." He might have pushed his snout against her face, but the motion was so weak, she could've imagined it.

Her eyes felt hot and gritty as she maneuvered the car back onto the roadway. Everything from finding the car's petrol filler to counting out unfamiliar money from Lars' wallet taxed her overburdened brain. She was running on sheer nerves, but she had to keep going. Had to get Lars to Garen. To help. She choked back the edges of hysteria.

Who the hell treated shifters? Sure and not emergency rooms. Not veterinarians, either.

She kept her voice calm, soothing, and called Lars' name.

"I am still on this side of the veil, fraulein. I heard you on the phone a while back. Excellent call. Garen is a good man. Solid."

"Hush, love. Don't be trying to talk. Just hang in there."

DAWN WAS BREAKING, illuminating jagged mountaintops with shades of pink, when she pulled into farm country at the outskirts of Idaho Falls. She hadn't had any further conversations with Lars, but the steady sound of his breathing filled her with hope. The cell phone jangled. When she uncrimped her fingers from the steering wheel to answer it, she understood how close to the edge she was.

"I see the car," Garen said without preamble. "Take the next exit, turn right, and drive to the end of whatever road you're on. I'll rendezvous with you there."

She dropped the phone back into the console and ferried the car off the highway. "You hear that, my sweet, my love. Garen's here. You're almost safe."

"No, *liebchen*, we're almost safe."

She was so shocked to hear his out loud voice, she almost plowed into a parked car. "Oh my God. When did you shift back?"

"Only a few moments ago. I was too weak until then. Had to get the bullet out first. Then my cat took more time than I would have liked to start healing the damage."

Tears coursed down her face. It was hard to breathe around the thickening in her throat. Lars was alive. He'd made it. Somehow, she ferried the car to a stop at the end of a deserted road, slammed on the parking brake, and got out. She yanked open the back door and stopped dead.

Blood. There was so much blood. How could he still be alive?

"It looks worse than it is. Happened while my cat extruded the bullet." He got out of the car shakily, and she wrapped her arms around him, never wanting to let go. Tamara tried to talk, but she was beyond words as she ran her hands up and down his body, reassuring herself he was whole.

"You're naked as a newborn babe. We have to be finding you something to put on."

"If that means I have to let go of you, I can skip it." His voice was a husky growl as he nuzzled her ear.

Tamara leaned her head against his chest, savoring the steady beat of his heart beneath her ear. She reluctantly disengaged herself and rummaged in the back of the car. Thank all the fucking saints his clothes weren't soaked with blood. She handed him things and helped him dress.

She'd just steadied him while he stepped into his shoes when the *whump-whump* of chopper blades descended toward them. One moment the helicopter was in the air, the next it had settled to the ground in a cloud of dust. A man emerged, bent low against the prop wash, and ran toward them. A woman exited the chopper right behind him, an imposing looking rifle slung over one shoulder. Once clear of the spinning rotors, she shouldered the gun and moved it in a slow arc. Tamara understood it had to be Miranda covering her mate—and them.

Garen wrapped his arms around both of them. "Not bad for a dead man." He clapped Lars on the back.

"As one much greater than I once said, the rumors of my death have been greatly exaggerated."

Lars leaned into Garen, and Tamara caught the barest glimpse of the depth of their relationship. It warmed her.

"I'd love to catch up," Garen said, his blue eyes twinkling in a face with pronounced bone structure, "but we can do that once we're airborne. Clear everything out of the rental car." He pulled a watch cap more firmly over longish salt-and-pepper hair.

"Sure and I'll take care of that," Tamara said, casting a concerned eye at Lars.

"Can you walk to the chopper?" Garen asked Lars.

"Of course."

"Then go. Your woman and I will clear the car."

Lars rubbed his cheek against Tamara's, turned, and walked slowly toward the helicopter. When he got to Miranda's side, she left her sentinel post long enough to help him.

"Now you know he's safe, move quick. We need to get out of here," Garen instructed.

Tamara scrambled back into the car, gathered everything that belonged to them, and tossed it outside into a pile. Once she was done, she scooped up an armload, carted it to the helicopter, and went back for more. Between her and Garen, they were done in just a few trips.

Garen grabbed her arm and pushed her toward the helicopter. "Time to go."

"But the keys? What should I do with the keys?" She dangled them in his face. "It's bad enough the back seat's all bloody."

"Lock up. Keep the keys. If luck is with us, the rental agency will only have to do a bit of cleanup, but I suspect they'll find the SUV either torched or full of bullet holes."

Tamara ran back to the car, slammed the doors, and hit the clicker. Remembering Lars' phone, still buried deep in the console, she unlocked the car, retrieved it, and sprinted for the helicopter.

Fear bit deep, making her legs shake. Garen's words had served as an unpleasant reminder that the world she knew was gone. Poof. Evaporated like mist on a morning bog. By the time she got to the chopper, everyone was inside but her. She pulled herself up the metal steps and moved out of the way so Miranda could shut and latch the door.

Miranda shoved black hair with white-blonde streaks over her shoulders and half lifted Tamara into a seat. When she struggled with the seatbelt because her hands shook so badly, Miranda fastened it for her.

"There now." The tall woman's voice was low and soothing, her blue eyes kind. "Everything will be fine."

Tamara tried to thank her, but all that emerged was a jumble of Irish. The world tilted and spun. Part of it was the helicopter lifting off, but part of it was her body finally hitting a breaking point.

"Aw, crap." Miranda's voice seemed to be coming from the bottom of a deep well. "Damn if she's not going to faint."

"She has every right," Lars said, pride shining in his words. "Even though she was scared out of her skin, she took care of business and killed two of the men who attacked us. Not just killed, shredded them."

"You hear that?" Miranda squeezed her shoulder. "You were a hero today. Strong work!"

Darkness swirled closer and closer. She heard Garen murmur, "Sounds like you've found yourself a keeper," just before everything shaded to black.

CHAPTER 13

"Goddammit!" Lars bent over Tamara. Anxiety soured his stomach. He reached a tentative hand and smoothed tangled, dark strands back from her face. *"Liebchen.* Come back to us. We are safe now." Despite his earlier words, having her unconscious rattled him.

"She'll be all right," Miranda said and patted his shoulder. "She only fainted. It will give her mind and body a mini-break."

His fears marginally alleviated, Lars settled into the seat opposite Tamara. Miranda lurched past him and half fell into the copilot's seat.

"Sorry," Garen said, his voice tight. "I wanted us out of there before anyone, friend or foe, showed up. So far, we've been lucky. No one's hit me up on the radio complaining we're off course for the flight plan I filed. Radar dude must be banging the office secretary this morning."

"What happened to you guys?" Miranda asked as she strapped herself in, settled a headset in place, and handed one back to Lars.

He put on the headset so they could talk over the roar of the dual rotors without shouting. "Jaret Chen's gang is as determined as the plague. One of the most recent batch they sent to kill us said something curious, though. Apparently they want me more than they want Tamara."

"Why would that be a surprise?" Garen asked, his hands and feet busy at the controls. "We've had more than our share of run-ins with them. Hell, you were supposed to terminate Chen."

Lars shrugged. "Maybe I deluded myself I was invisible to them. It took a while, but I remembered the American—"

"What American?" Miranda asked.

"Sorry. Let me back up." Lars hit the high points about the latest attack. "...Anyway, I should have found something to tie to the rear bumper to obliterate our tracks on the dirt road. As it was, I may as well have hung out a sign, LARS AND TAMARA WENT THIS WAY."

"The American," Garen prodded.

"*Ja.* I fought him in Sudan. He probably saw me shift, but all he said earlier was I had an *affinity* for big cats."

"Was that the time Garen told me about when you got a pride of lions to help out?" Miranda asked.

Lars chuckled. "One of my finer moments. Those cats could have torn me to bits. That they did not will remain one of the unsolved mysteries."

"Now that the nitty-gritty stuff is out of the way," Miranda went on, "tell us about Tamara." Something distinctly feminine, at odds with her espionage persona, slithered beneath her words.

Lars glanced at Tamara's inert form and reached over to lay a protective hand on her arm. "She is special."

"Oooh, don't tell me you might be falling in love." Miranda jabbed Garen in the ribs. "It's the stellar example we set."

"Do not jump the gun, *fraulein,*" Lars said to Miranda. "The lady and I have had very little time to get to know one another when we have not been running for our lives."

"That's the very best time to assess someone's mettle," Garen cut in. "See what they're made of. From what I can tell, your Tamara is one tough bitch."

Lars bit back a laugh. "She is not *my Tamara*, though I might wish her to be."

"I wouldn't be so certain of that," Garen retorted. "She called me because she was desperately afraid for you."

"She would have done the same for anyone," Lars insisted. "After all, I stepped in and helped her in Nice. She is grateful…"

"Why is it so threatening for you to get your confirmed bachelor mind around romance?" Miranda smirked. "I heard her on the phone, and saw her in your arms when we landed. If that's not a woman in love, I don't know what is."

Tamara made a gurgling noise and stirred. Lars unsnapped his seat belt, moved across the slender aisle, and knelt by her side. "*Liebchen.*" He stroked the side of her face. "Can I get you something? Anything? Water, juice, crackers?"

"Sure and a good, stiff shot of Irish whiskey would set well," she mumbled.

"Aha!" Miranda said. "She's back with the living. Here." She handed another headset over. "Give her this. I don't want to miss anything. What'd she ask for?"

Tamara opened her eyes and grinned as she adjusted the headset over her head. "Whiskey. I asked for spirits. Are there any aboard? I can hear you fine even without these." She tapped the headset. "Or my cat can."

"Yeah," Miranda said. "I'd forgotten. They have better ears than wolves."

"Is that what you are?" Tamara clapped a hand over her mouth. "Sure and it's sorry I am. It's not polite to be discussing such things."

"You can talk about anything you'd like here. You're in good company," Garen assured her. "We band together so we can be who we are—all of who we are."

"To answer your question—" Miranda shot Garen a pointed look "—he and I are both wolves. Everyone who works for Rubicon International is a shifter. There are a few bears, a coyote or two, lots of wolves, and lots of mountain lions. We normally don't share that type of information, but given we already know you're one of us, I decided to bend that rule—"

"I already told her that." Lars broke into Miranda's explanation.

Concern for Tamara tied his gut into a tight knot. She'd been through a hell of a lot. "How are you feeling?"

"Not bad." She paused for a beat. "So long as I don't think too hard or too deep about what happened."

Lars got back into his seat, buckled in, and reached for her hand. She gripped it tightly. "Are there spirits aboard?" he asked Garen.

He shook his head. "We could land in Spokane and have breakfast, or I can just take us home."

"Which would you prefer?" Lars squeezed her hand.

She opened her mouth just before her face crumpled and tears welled. She wrenched her hand out of his, dropped her head into her hands, and sobbed.

"Did I say something wrong, *liebchen?*" His heart ached, but he felt confused too. All he'd asked was what she wanted to do.

He glanced at Miranda, but she mouthed, "Give her a moment."

"Not you." Tamara's voice was muffled. She swiped at her face and raised her head. "It was hearing the word *home*, and thinking I'll never have one again. Sorry. God, but I'm a maudlin mess. With a wee bit of sleep, sure and I'll be more myself."

"Sweetie." Miranda's voice was sharp through the headsets. "You've been through hell. You have zilch in the way of training as a field agent, yet you've operated as one ever since you terminated Chen. Probably before that too, since you infiltrated his operation and defenses to get yourself into position to off him. Give yourself a break. Have a meltdown. You've earned the right. We train for years to accomplish what you did."

Lars got out of his seat again, knelt beside Tamara, and pulled her into his arms. "You will always have a home with me, *liebchen*. I know we do not know one another well, but—"

"What was that you said?" she squeaked. "Sure and you're acting right daft. You scarcely know me. I might be a witch by night."

"Then you will be my witch." He kissed her forehead.

Miranda cried, "Bravo!" and clapped her hands together.

"You'll have to forgive my mate," Garen said. "She always did have a flair for drama."

"Nothing quite like a four-way proposal." Lars snorted. "Could the two of you zip it long enough for me to talk with Tamara?"

"As long as we can listen." Miranda chuckled.

Garen glanced over one shoulder and winked at Lars. "Sorry, Miranda's a hopeless romantic."

"Hey!" She elbowed him. "I picked you, didn't I?"

"We picked each other," Garen pointed out smugly.

"Shut up!" Lars let go of Tamara long enough to mock punch both of them.

"How about this?" Tamara tugged off her headset and turned it off.

"Excellent idea." Lars did the same. The chopper's rough floor made his knees ache, but he wouldn't have left Tamara's side if he'd been kneeling on knives.

"Did you really mean that? About home?" Her blue eyes flooded again.

He drew back so their gazes met. "Yes. I meant it." She opened her mouth, but he laid a hand over it. "You were incredibly brave and resourceful. You got me into the car and us out of there. Had we stayed, more men would have shown up."

"It has to be more than you thinking I'd make a good field agent."

He swallowed hard. "It is. I am not very good at talking about matters of the heart, but something about you called to me from the very first moment I saw you huddled in the back of that taxi."

She smiled. "They call that sex, and the fascination is mutual. I could scarcely wait to get my hands under your clothes."

Lars shook his head. "The physical attraction is strong, but it is much more than that. I cannot get enough of you." His face heated, but he forged ahead anyway. "Before with women, I left as soon as things were finished. With you, it is different."

She stroked the side of his face. "I want to believe you—because I feel the same way."

"I would not lie to you, *liebchen*. Maybe because I have lived so long—" his blush deepened "—and shared my bed with so many women, I recognize that what we have is different, special." He gathered her body into his arms again. Maybe he shouldn't have mentioned *other women*, but she melted against him.

"Tell you what," she said. "Let's be getting a spot of distance between us and disaster. Maybe waking up together, having a meal or two…" Her voice ran down.

He brushed his lips over the top of her head and got creakily to his feet. The gunshot wound had taken a toll, one that would take at least a few more hours to move past. "We can do this any way you wish, *liebchen*. So long as I have you near me, that is all I care about."

He moved back into his seat, resettled his headset, and handed Tamara hers.

"Well?" Miranda spun in her seat to gaze expectantly at them. "Do I get to plan a wedding?"

Lars held his breath. When Tamara said, "Maybe," his heart took flight.

~

THE HELICOPTER SETTLED on the roof of Garen's Capitol Hill mansion in Seattle with barely a shudder. Lars helped Tamara out and led the way into a house he knew almost as well as his own.

"This is Garen's home?" Tamara's eyes widened as Lars steered her down richly carpeted stairs to the room on the second floor where he always stayed. "Sure and it could be a museum with all the paintings and sculptures and—" She stopped dead right in front of a bronze statue of a wolf with a man kneeling by his side. Tamara grazed her fingertips over the glowing metal and turned to Lars. "Whoever made this was exceptionally talented. They look alive."

"Garen has had many years to collect beautiful things. I am anxious to share my home in Heidelberg with you."

"Is it grand like this?"

Lars considered the question. "It is difficult to assess how another's eyes will see something. I live in a manor house that was built in the sixteen hundreds. Of course, it has been modernized."

Tamara narrowed her eyes. "I'm thinking you've owned it for a long time."

"You would be correct." He grinned. "When a Prussian Count was killed, leaving no heirs, I bought it at auction. This way." He tugged open a door and gestured her inside a large, sunny room in the southwest corner of the house. A king-sized bed covered with a fluffy duvet nestled beneath dormer windows. Antique armoires and matching dressers made of a rich, dark wood lined two walls.

He set down his valise, computer case, and her suitcase, having left the clothing they'd bought for her in the helicopter. She held her arms out from her sides and twirled in place before running to the window and looking outside.

"The gardens are incredible." She turned slowly and faced him. "It's all a wee bit overwhelming. I've led a simple life. Not that I've ever been truly poor, mind you, but nor has there ever been much left over."

"Do you think you will be comfortable here?"

"Oh my, yes. It's as if I've died and been reborn somewhere better."

A sharp tap sounded on the door just before Garen opened it, with Miranda right behind him. "We're going to get something going for a late breakfast. Care to join us?" he asked.

"What do you think?" Lars turned to Tamara.

"Might I clean up a bit first?"

"Of course," Miranda piped up, adding, "Do you like hot water?"

"Sure and it's better than cold."

Miranda laughed heartily. "Not quite what I meant. Come with me. We'll just pop into the spa. There's a hot tub and a sauna and a lap pool. By the time we're done, the boys will have something edible on hand." She eyed Garen. "Won't you?"

"Sure, darling. Even if I have to order it."

"I can cook," Tamara murmured.

"You're our guest," Miranda said firmly. "No cooking required. Come on." She crooked a finger. "I'd love to get to know you better. You can tell me all about Ireland."

Lars watched as the two women walked out of the bedroom and down the hall toward the spa in the basement. He waited until they were out of sight and quirked a brow at Garen. "That felt staged. What do you need to tell me?"

"Aw, shit. Am I that transparent?"

"Not to the fair *fraulein*, but I have known you for a very long time. Something has happened. Tell me."

"I got hold of the car rental agency. By the time they sent someone to collect their car, it was peppered with bullet holes."

"I will reimburse you."

"Not my point. Collateral damage and all that. A much bigger problem is we're embroiled in an all-out war. We need to strike hard and fast to make them think twice about continuing to harass us."

"Damn it. I had feared something of this magnitude would occur when those men tracked us from the Casper airport." Lars took a quick inventory of his body. "Give me a few hours to sleep and eat, and then I will be ready to—"

Garen shook his head. "I've already deployed troops. You need to heal. Tamara needs a few days when she isn't worried sick you'll come home in a box."

"But this is my battle," Lars protested.

"No, old friend." Garen borrowed one of Lars' favorite appellations. "It is *our* battle. You may yet be conscripted, but for now you've done your part."

"What exactly are we doing?"

Garen's somber expression shifted into a vicious grin. "What else? We've targeted two of the plants where they produce heroin." He glanced at his watch. "Bombs should be exploding any minute now."

"Damn! Guess we play hardball. I am glad to be on our side."

"I wouldn't have it any other way, old buddy." Garen shot a mock frown his way. "If you ever even think about switching camps, I'll hunt you down and make you sorry you were ever born."

Lars cocked his head to one side. "I do not believe you have much to concern yourself with on that front." He slugged Garen in the bicep. Garen hit him back, and they grappled with one another for long moments before dissolving into laughter.

Lars loped into the adjoining bathroom and splashed cold water on his face. When he walked back into the bedroom, he said, "You have delivered your message. What is Miranda talking with Tamara about?"

"Do you even have to ask?" Garen clapped Lars on the back.

Lars rolled his eyes. "Probably not. She is signing her on with Rubicon International."

"Exactly. Grab something that doesn't reek of blood and come help me in the kitchen."

Lars unbuttoned his shirt, toed off his shoes, and unzipped his pants. He tossed the dirty clothes in a pile. Garen whistled long and low. "What?" Lars demanded.

"Stand in front of the mirror and see for yourself."

Lars moved in front of the wall-mounted mirror, and his eyes widened at his reflection. "Fuck. It is worse than I imagined." His entire abdomen was black and blue with a perforated scar to the right of his belly button. Glancing down, he assessed his injury with a critical eye. "At least it is healing well."

"Cats do have nine lives."

"Best hope I have a few more than that, old friend, else I would have been dead long since." Lars snapped up a pale green polo shirt from a dresser drawer, tugged it over his head, and went hunting for a pair of sweat pants and some slippers. "By the way, what is for breakfast?"

"Scrambled eggs and coffee."

"Works for me." Lars followed Garen downstairs to the kitchen.

"Yeah, well, the ladies might want something more elegant."

"So?" Lars shrugged. "We can call that bakery and order something. I will take care of that part."

CHAPTER 14

Tamara took another slug of excellent coffee and folded her hands over her stomach. "It's full and then some I am. Thank you boys for breakfast."

"Quite a spread." Miranda nodded appreciatively. "I could've sworn we'd be stuck with coffee and eggs."

"You married a man of many talents." Garen winked at his mate.

"Don't start listing them, for chrissakes." She made a strangled sound as if she was choking back laughter. "Seriously, thanks for cooking—and for not grilling Tam and me while we ate."

"Since you brought it up—" Garen's words were cut short by a blast from his cell phone. He fished it out of a pocket and barked, "Report," while pushing his chair back and loping out of the sunny breakfast nook. It was separated by swinging doors from a kitchen with so many stainless steel appliances they'd nearly blinded Tamara.

Lars and Miranda fairly bristled with tension, their gazes glued to the still moving swinging door Garen had disappeared through.

"What is it I don't know about?" Tamara asked. The breakfast she'd just consumed turned to a leaden block in her belly.

Garen strode back into the breakfast nook flashing a thumbs-up sign. Lars and Miranda broke into broad grins. "Score one for our side." Miranda fist-pumped the air.

"Yes, those bastards will be so busy rebuilding, they will not have anyone left over to send after us." Lars looked grimly satisfied.

"Will one of you be telling me what the fuck is going on?" Tamara heard a shrill note she didn't care for in her voice, but she hated being odd man out.

Miranda shifted her chair and settled her gaze on Tamara. "You remember that conversation we had down in the spa?"

"Of course."

Miranda quirked a dark brow. It cut across her tanned forehead like a bird's wing. "Well?"

Tamara blew out a tense breath. She'd known she'd have to make a decision.

What? Was I hoping I'd have a spot more time? Nothing will change, even if I had months.

Lars laid a hand over one of hers. "It is all right, *liebchen*. Take your time. It is a big decision. I will not think less of you if—"

She waved him to silence and smiled weakly. "Sure and you're babbling. Never would have thought you'd be the type. I appreciate your concern, and your caring." She shifted her focus to Miranda and Garen. "I'm still not understanding why you'd want me to be a part of Rubicon International. I understand why Lars would, but not the two of you. I have nothing much to offer."

"Let me be the judge of that." Garen matched the seriousness of her tone. "I've been recruiting agents for a long time. You definitely have the right stuff."

"You'll have to work hard, develop enough skills so you feel confident, rather than terrified," Miranda cut in.

"We wouldn't rush you," Garen said. "It normally takes a couple of years to train a field agent."

Tamara laced her hands around her coffee cup. "So I'd be dead weight for two years? I'm not liking the sound of that."

"Not at all," Miranda said. "We always have agents at all stages of training. We consider it insurance, not *dead weight*."

"Could I keep on writing—assuming I found newspapers around here I could freelance for?"

"Under a different name," Garen said, "but that shouldn't pose a problem since you'll need several alternate identifications."

Tamara swallowed more coffee. The next question was hard, but she had to know. "My family. Will they have to think I'm dead?"

"Aw, sweetie." Miranda lunged halfway across the table and patted her shoulder. "Of course not."

"But won't it be dangerous for them if they know I'm alive and where I am?"

"Who are your parents?" Garen asked. "I did some research, and narrowed it down to two possible shifter families."

"Leona and Christian MacBride," Tamara replied, mystified. "Why are their names important?"

Garen drew his brows together into a thin line. "I may know your father. He's been around for a while, hasn't he?"

"If you're asking whether he's one of the old ones, he is." Tamara pressed her lips together. "He deals in jewelry. He's not some kind of revolutionary. Sure and I'd know after all the tragedies I covered in Northern Ireland."

"That would be in your lifetime," Garen said softly. "Unless he told you, you'd have no idea who—or what—he was before."

Lars, who'd been uncharacteristically quiet, took her hand again. "I have been thinking—"

"Uh-oh." Garen snorted. "Always dangerous."

"Ssht," Miranda said. "Let's see what he came up with."

"Thank you." Lars inclined his head toward Miranda. "We must proceed in some sort of order—"

"Watch it!" Garen stabbed a finger toward Lars. "Your German roots are showing."

Lars rolled his eyes. "The order is this, or it could be if Tamara wishes. First, she must decide whether she will sign on with

Rubicon International." He turned his gray gaze on Miranda. "Did you tell her everything? That this is a lifetime commitment with no out-clause?"

Miranda nodded solemnly. "Yup. I covered all the bases. Normally, we don't let our agents know that part until after their final test, but given the circumstances—and the fact she already knows many of the secrets we withhold from all but our fully vetted agents—I made certain she knew that also."

"Excellent." Lars smiled warmly. "Once she decides, then we will bind her with the blood oath, even though she is not yet a vetted agent." Garen opened his mouth, but Lars shook his head. "Hear me out. We already know she is one of us. The only reason to withhold the blood oath is because you wait until the very last moment to assure yourself your agents are shifters. A tactic I strongly disagree with, by the way."

"Yes, you've said as much," Garen muttered and made a grab for his coffee.

"She will be safer after the blood oath because it allows telepathic communication among us in human form," Lars argued. "And over distances."

"He has a point," Miranda said.

"From my own mate?" Garen tried to look upset, but the corners of his mouth twitched.

"We're all part of a board of directors that runs Rubicon International," she pointed out. "If we want to change some aspects of how we do things, we put it to the board for a vote."

"Mmph. Guess I did agree to that." Garen's twitching mouth curved into a grin. "It will take some getting used to, since I'm accustomed to running things."

"Yes, well I was used to running the European office." Lars shrugged. "Time marches on, my friend. But we digress. Back to Tamara." He moved his chair right next to her and draped an arm around her shoulders. "Many game pieces will fall into place, but the linchpin is your decision about Rubicon International. We cannot finish this conversation until you have made up your mind."

"May I get up? Walk around a bit by myself, maybe out in those lovely gardens."

"Of course." Lars got to his feet and held a hand to her. "You will probably want a jacket. It is not as warm as it appears. The grounds are safe."

"I had a feeling they'd be." She wanted to bury herself in his arms. Instead she walked straight-backed from the kitchen table. A clear head would be her ally, and Lars clouded her thoughts. According to him, she'd be a part of his life no matter what, but she had a feeling things would be different, richer, deeper, if she signed on with Rubicon International.

For one thing, I'd know what they were all so thrilled about when Garen did that thumbs-up deal.

Tamara reached the top of the stairs and headed for their room. She found her jacket easily enough, slid it on, and retraced her steps, except this time she let herself out the ornate front door. As she walked down brick steps and wandered through a garden laid out in rectangular and circular planting beds, she made an effort to sort her jumbled thoughts.

Part of the problem was she hadn't totally moved past feeling like Jaret Chen's patsy. Her escape had slid from a sure thing, to dicey, to little shy of miraculous after Lars dragged her out of the taxi. Tamara asked herself what sort of woman would place herself in that kind of situation. Did the fact that she had mean she had the raw material she'd need to work in espionage?

What Garen had inferred about her father was intriguing. Tamara didn't know much about either parent, beyond who they'd been raising her and her siblings. It was almost as if her family had a *don't ask, don't tell* policy in place, sort of like the U.S. military for their gay soldiers.

About the only thing I know is they raised other kids. We never did find out about our older brothers and sisters because it was too dangerous...

One of the huge pluses of signing on with Rubicon International would be being able to claim all of who she was. To not have to hide anymore. Shifters who admitted what they were had been forced into compounds—or killed outright. They wore electronic ankle bands to track their movements. At first, it had been just in the United States, but Canada, Europe, and the U.K. were quick to pass similar laws. All that happened before she'd been born—except the electronic ankle band part—so she'd never lived in a time when she didn't have to lead a dual existence.

She sat on a stone bench and inhaled the mingled scents of damp flowers and greenery. The Pacific Northwest was rainy and verdant. In many ways, it reminded her of Ireland. Deeper thoughts pricked her. She'd known at some level she'd never be able to go home once Jaret was dead. She hadn't allowed herself to go there because it might've crippled her resolve.

Maybe I'm more like Lars and Garen and Miranda than I know...

Tamara got to her feet and made her way back into the house. The group wasn't in the cozy breakfast nook anymore. It didn't take her long to locate them in another of the home's many downstairs rooms. She walked through the door of a cheerful sitting room with a stone fireplace at one end. Colorful occasional chairs and sofas were scattered in small conversational groupings. Floor-to-ceiling bookshelves lined two walls. Lars, Tamara, and Garen turned at the sound of her footsteps.

Lars bolted to his feet, his heart in his eyes. He held out both hands to her, but she shook her head. "Sure and you're an amazing man, but my head is clear and I don't want to muddy things. It's kind of you to invite me to be a part of what you've been building for a long time." She stopped to take a measured breath, blew it out, and took another.

"I thought about a lot of things while I was outside, but maybe the biggest one is I'm sick of feeling like a second-class citizen, of pretending to be what I'm not. So—" she looked right at Lars "—

regardless of whether you and I end up together, I accept the offer to sign on with Rubicon."

Miranda whooped. She jumped out of her chair, ran to Tamara, and swept her into a huge hug. "Enjoy the love now," she said through laughter. "I'm a bitch in the field."

Garen shoved his mate aside and shook Tamara's hand. "Welcome aboard." Miranda looped an arm through Garen's and pulled hard. He looked at his mate. "What?"

"They need to talk," she said pointedly and dragged Garen out of the sitting room.

LARS STILL HAD his hands extended toward her, but he felt suddenly shy and awkward, and dropped them to his sides. "*Ja*. Miranda is correct. There is much to talk about. Would you like to sit? Or maybe walk a little more? You never did take your coat off."

"So I didn't. Sure and walking would be perfect." She turned and strode out of the room.

He followed her, wanting to touch her, at least hold her hand, but he understood she had to come to him. He caught up to her at the front door and held it open.

"Such a gentleman," she murmured.

"It is the time I came from. Men were trained to care for women then. It was ingrained."

She set a moderate pace. He walked by her side. A light rain fell, more of a mist than anything. "What happens next?" she asked.

"For us, or for you and Rubicon International?"

She stopped a moment, her forehead creased in thought. "Both. Start with Rubicon International. That one is more straightforward. Come on." She brushed damp hair back from her face. "Easier to talk when we're on the move."

He fell into step next to her again. "You will share blood with Garen, and then we will develop a training regimen for you. It will be similar to a job. You will have a schedule to increase your physical endurance and to teach you skills that are effective in the field." He took a breath. "There are milestones. When you have accomplished a minimum amount of them, we will give you your first assignment." He couldn't keep a fond smile off his face. "Much of it will feel trivial after the things you have already done."

"What were Garen and the rest of you so stoked about earlier?"

Lars started to relay an annotated history of their war with Chen's gang, decided it was overkill, and settled for saying, "We had to do something to make Chen's people back off, so Garen deployed agents to destroy two of the labs where they refine poppy juice into heroin."

She halted and turned so she faced him. "Sure and it can't be that easy." She snapped her fingers. "You blow up a lab and they go away."

"It is not. But we did slow them down. Their priority will be to rebuild, so they will leave us alone—for now." He inhaled sharply. "The war is never over, *liebchen*. There will always be bad guys."

"What you do is important work."

He placed a finger beneath her chin. "What *we* do is important work. You are one of us now."

"So I am. It will be taking a wee bit of time for that to sink in." She licked her lips, her gaze somber. "Now. About us."

"I am falling in love with you." Shock waves rocked him to his conservative core. Was it possible he'd actually said that?

"You've got that just-swallowed-an-elephant look about you again."

"Probably, but it is because such things do not come easily to me. I will care for you, *liebchen*. Protect you. Love you. Shelter our children from harm."

Her eyes glistened with unshed tears. She closed the distance between them, and he folded her into his arms, rejoicing in the feel of her body against him. He wanted to kiss her until they were both breathless, and do a whole lot more beyond that, but he satisfied himself with her body molded to his and her scent eddying about them. They weren't quite done talking. He had good news and wanted to make certain she knew because it might set her mind at ease.

"Garen checked his records. They helped him home in on just which MacBride family you belonged to. Once he'd done that, he remembered some things about your father."

"Really?" She drew away, curiosity burning in her eyes.

He nodded, "Really. Come, *liebchen*. There is an enclosed gazebo at the end of this walkway with a brazier I can light if you are cold. It will be more comfortable and get us out of the rain."

She took his hand while they navigated the inlaid brick walkway past a fountain and up a few steps. He opened the summerhouse door and dusted off cushions that sat on a bench built into one wall. The air smelled damp, so he fired the electric brazier. In short order, it glowed cherry red from its raised, round dais in the center of the room.

He sat with his back against the wall and his feet propped on the stove's platform. She curled her body against him. He sensed her waiting for him to say more. "Most of this is not my story to tell. You must ask your father. He worked with Garen for well over a hundred years, both in the Old Country and here in the United States."

She twisted so she could look at him. "Da was a…a spy?"

Lars nodded. "He was. So he will understand and support you in your new occupation."

Her forehead creased in concentration, and she closed her teeth over her lower lip. "It also means he can keep Mum and everyone safe." She blew out a tense breath. "Och and that was one of the things that worried me the most, once the deed was done and Jaret was dead. I was scared silly my hare-brained scheme to avenge Moira would mean someone would come after my family. There would've been no living with myself if something happened to them because I was rash and stupid."

He kissed her forehead and smoothed the concern from it with a gentle hand. "Your father can take care of himself and his loved ones. Bet on it."

"Why wouldn't he have said anything?" She shook her head. "Never mind. I know the answer. It's the same reason we shied away from anything related to being shifters."

"So long as you brought that up—" Lars settled a hand in her hair, drawing her thick locks through his fingers "—there is one more thing."

"What might that be?"

"I asked you once, half in jest, if your family taught you anything about shifters and mating."

"Yes, I remember."

"You come from old stock, as do I. There are other types of shifters, like those who become lycans when someone bites them. It is different for them than for those of us who inherit our dual form. There are also wolf shifters who are not lycan. Their magic is weaker than ours."

"You're telling me this for a reason, but for the life of me, I'm not sorting it out."

"That is because I am not being very clear. Let me start over." He pulled her head against his chest and caressed it, loving the feel of her hair and of her next to him. "The shifter mate bond is a gift we old ones bear. It is why I am so drawn to you, and you to me, even before we make love in both our forms. It will take time for you to accept, but you are the only woman for me. And I the only man for you."

"What if I hadn't shown up?"

"I gave up on finding my mate long ago, gave up on having children. I am still astonished our paths crossed. To answer you more directly, if I had not met you, I would have continued as I was. My work was my life. At times it was almost enough, and when it was not, I volunteered for particularly dangerous assignments to drive my loneliness away."

"Well and that clears up why I never could make things stick with a boyfriend." She snuggled closer. "Mum tried to tell me that, but I never believed her. It feels so right being in your arms, but it's like a miracle too, and it's damned hard to believe in them. Not since I grew up, anyway."

They sat for long moments with her cradled against him. He knew what he wanted, what he needed. Before he could get the words out, she said, "Today is a day for chances. If you're willing, I'd like for us to shift and make love."

His heart cracked and spilled over. Tears were closer to the surface than they'd been since he was a boy. She moved away from him, placed a hand on either side of his face, and closed her mouth over his. He read love and longing in her kiss, along with heat and hope as she nibbled, licked, and suckled his tongue.

His cock swelled, desperate to take her, make her his forever. He broke their kiss. "Are you certain?"

She smiled, her lips flower-petal soft from their kiss. "Yes, I've never been more so."

CHAPTER 15

*L*ars had just enough presence of mind to shut off the brazier. He turned to Tamara and began to undress her, starting with her shoes. He rubbed the insteps of her feet, and she wriggled her toes against his hands, making little mewing noises. He ran his hands up her ankles and calves, enjoying the feel of her sleekly muscled legs, before unfastening her pants.

"Dear God, but your hands feel heavenly." She smiled dreamily. "It's almost painful to tear myself away, but this will be easier if we stand." She got to her feet, and her pants pooled around her. She stepped out of them and reached for the waistband of his sweats, running a palm over his hard-on. He leaned into her, wanting her to touch him, and she did, but only for a moment. She slid his sweatpants over his hips with firm hands, followed by his shorts. His cock sprang free. Tamara's fingers hovered so close, he felt the heat of them, but she made a grab for the bottom of his shirt instead and tugged it upward.

He realized he still had his slippers on and worked his way out of them, so he could untangle himself from the welter of pants and underwear around his feet. While his face was buried in his shirt, something hot and electric moved across his chest. Her mouth. She kissed his nipples, sending a jolt of white heat to his groin. He escaped from the shirt and tossed it onto a seat.

"If you do much more of that, we will never make it to our cat forms."

She looked up at him, beautiful in muted light that played through the gazebo windows. "I've never done that before."

He was so hot, thinking wasn't easy. "Done what?" His tongue felt thick and uncooperative.

"Made love in my other form." She cocked her head to one side. "Have you?"

"Yes, but not with another shifter. I have sometimes spent months as a cat, living as they do."

She tilted her chin up. "You'll be helping me? I…"

"Your cat will know what to do. Trust her."

"I don't know." Tamara grinned ruefully. "She's been mighty quiet these past few minutes. No clamoring to get out. No commentary at all."

He spanned her waist, reveling in her silky skin, and then moved upward to tease her breasts. Warm and firm, with pebbled nipples, they felt as if they belonged in his hands. She moaned and pressed into his touch. Sandwiched between their bodies, his cock twitched and jumped, reminding him of its need.

He unzipped her jacket. Once it was off her shoulders, he pulled her stretchy top over her head and opened his arms. She wrapped hers around him and turned her face up for a kiss. He wanted everything. Kissing, hugging, fondling, fucking. He sank his tongue into her mouth, and she sparred with it. Without breaking their kiss, he ran his hands down her naked back, found the taut globes of her ass, and pulled her hard against his erection. Lars groaned at her proximity because she felt so goddamned good. No one had ever felt like that before. Like they'd been born to be a part of him.

His breathing quickened as the mate bond spun its magic. The woman in his arms was everything he'd ever dreamed of. Reluctantly, he lifted his mouth from hers. "It is time," he said, his voice harsh with passion and unfulfilled need.

She stepped back, and the air around her shimmered as the sleek form of her mountain cat emerged. She padded around him, sniffing enthusiastically. On the second transit, she rasped her sandpaper tongue over his burning erection.

He laughed. "If that is not a *hurry up*, I have never been on the receiving end of one. We can move out of doors, *liebchen*. The garden fence is solid. It will shroud us from view."

He crossed the room in a single stride and pushed the door open. Tamara leapt through, made an acrobatic midair twist, and ended on all fours facing him, her tongue lolling. Lars reached for his cat from. Unlike Tamara's cat, his had been champing at the bit for freedom. He knew what was about to happen and couldn't wait.

Lars rubbed noses with Tamara. His cock was so taut, butting from its furred sheath, it was almost uncomfortable. He licked her snout. She licked back and then wove her head between his back legs and licked him shamelessly. The heat was so intense, he almost came. His cat jerked away from her questing tongue and licked her vulva. Things spun out of control fast after that. Animal sex wasn't complicated. No foreplay. No hands to smooth or fingers to explore.

She planted her feet firmly and twisted her tail out of the way. He mounted her, sank his teeth into the side of her neck, and drove his cock all the way inside. The heat of her closing around him made him crazy with lust. Semen jetted out almost immediately, and kept on pumping.

She tilted her head back, yowling and screeching as a climax ripped through her. He plumbed her deeper, and she contracted her muscles around him. They stood joined for long moments. He licked the place he'd bitten her neck. She twisted her head and licked his mouth.

"We must remain like this until my erection goes down, liebchen."

"Why?"

"Cat cocks have barbs. I will hurt you if I withdraw when I am this hard."

She arched beneath him. He shifted more of his weight to his hind legs and listened while his cat and Tamara's crooned to one another. It was sweet and tender and totally unexpected. The tension in his cock finally lessened. He tugged gently to loosen its grip on her pussy.

Once they were free, she purred. The sound was deep and throaty and made him feel on top of the world. She nudged him with her snout, cried, *"Run with me,"* and took off through Garen's gated half-acre garden.

Lars bolted after her, impressed by both her speed and her agility. She weighed less than him by a good fifty or sixty pounds, and she led him a merry chase in, out, and around bushes, flowers, and decorative shrubs. When she finally drew to a halt, panting, her sides heaving, he dropped to his belly before her and rolled over in mock surrender. *"You win, liebchen."*

"I don't know about winning, but that was fun."

"Ready to be human again?"

When she nodded, he got to his feet, summoned magic and shifted. The air around her glistened with iridescent motes in the rain. Tamara stepped out of them, rosy and smiling, right into his arms.

"It was fun," he said. "It has been long since I played—at anything."

"Sure and life can be pretty grim. It helps to lighten things up." A shadow crossed her face. "Did I, er, was I all right?"

"You were perfect, love. I could not have asked for more. Did I hurt you?"

"A little, but I came so hard it was worth it." She looked thoughtful. "Sex is different that way. Hotter, more intense. After you licked my pussy, I couldn't have stopped if the world blew up around us."

He snorted. "I had a hell of a time not laying you down on that bench in the gazebo. You are beautiful, perfect, impossible to resist."

She shivered in his arms. "Brrr. I wasn't cold until just now. Better watch those compliments, I'll become unbearable."

"Somehow, I doubt that." He scooped her into his arms and carried her back to the gazebo. He wanted to make love to her again, but she had to be sore. Maybe they could dry off and curl up and sleep for a few hours.

He set her down once they were inside the summerhouse and rummaged for towels, finding some beneath the bench seats. He started to dry her, but she yanked the towel away. "Silly. I can manage."

"Maybe we could sleep for a bit."

"Och, and then eat, and then make love again." She shot him a coquettish grin. "I've got your number, big boy."

Lars set his towel down and eyed her. "If you ran the universe, how would you arrange the next few hours?"

"Let's see." She snapped her fingers. "Sure and I'd vote for a nap, maybe some decent spirits, and as much more of that—" she made a grab for his half-hard cock "—as I can get."

"Are you sore?"

She rubbed her thighs together experimentally. "Maybe a little, but not so much as to slow things down." She winked broadly. "We Irish are a randy bunch. It's the long winters and all those potatoes and free-flowing whiskey."

He sorted his clothes and began pulling them on. So did she. When they'd worked their way down to shoes and socks, she asked, "Is there any way I could be calling my folks? Sure and they're likely worried half to death about me since you killed my cell phone."

He snorted. "I suppose that would be one way to describe it. The terms we use in the field are *dismantle* or *deactivate*. I dismantled your phone, *liebchen*."

"I like my description better. It's more…colorful. You didn't answer my question."

"Every phone line in Garen's house is scrambled, so you can call your parents. It might be best if you did not tell them exactly where—"

"Give me credit for a wee bit of brains." She placed her hands on her hips. "It will be enough for them to know I'm alive and in good hands."

The rain, which had been pattering on the gazebo's roof, suddenly grew much louder. Lars glanced out a window. "Damn! Hail. Would you like me to run for an umbrella?"

"It's all right, Sir Galahad." She grinned. "Sure and I won't melt."

TAMARA CLIMBED the stairs inside Garen's house, with Lars right behind her. They'd run into Garen and Miranda after returning to the house during the hail storm. Garen had insisted on cracking a bottle of champagne to celebrate their mating, and Miranda immediately began planning their wedding. It wouldn't happen until June, so they had a few months, but Miranda assured her they'd need every minute of the time to attend to all the details. About all they'd decided was to hold the ceremony at Lars' home in Heidelberg.

They sat in the study for hours chatting until Tamara actually dozed off. Lars had excused them then and they were finally on their way to their room. She tried to think how long it had been since she'd had a night's sleep and couldn't come up with an answer. Certainly not since she'd killed Jaret, and that was going on a few days ago. Maybe more. She tried counting, but her brain felt fuzzy.

Lars opened the door to their room. She crossed under the lintel on autopilot and fell onto the bed, where he took her clothes off. She tried to help, but he batted her hands away and crooned to her in German.

"What are you saying?" she asked sleepily.

"That I love you. That you are very beautiful and very precious."

"It's the first thing I want to do."

"What is?" He addressed his own clothing, dropping it in a heap on a nearby chair.

"Learn German."

"Rubicon International has language tapes for almost every language."

"Sure and you would. Makes sense."

"What I speak is a dialect. Much of it has fallen out of usage, but if you tackle modern German, you will be able to understand most of my words. We can practice together, so long as you promise to help me with Irish." He pulled the window curtains and joined her in the large, comfy bed. She rolled into his arms and was asleep in moments.

When she woke, the room was truly dark, so much so she knew night had not only fallen, but moved past midnight. The gentle sound of Lars' breathing next to her was reassuring.

She reached for him and was surprised when he said, "You are awake, *liebchen.*"

"Yes, but how come you are?"

"I do not need much sleep." He rolled over and struck a match. The smell of sulfur was sharp for a moment, and then a candle flickered to life on his bedside table. She sat up and turned so she could look at him. His ice-blond hair was tousled from the pillow. His face, while still sharp planes and angles, looked softer somehow, and the depths of his gray eyes reflected twin flames from the candlelight.

She traced the line of his cheekbone down to his jaw. "I can't believe how lucky I was to find you. You're such a beautiful man. Kind and compassionate, even though you try to come off tough."

"What was that you said out in the gazebo? Something like, *I have your number.*" He grinned. It transformed his face into one that would've fit a mischievous imp. "Maybe my softer side can be our little secret. The men would never stop haranguing me if they overheard you yapping about *kind and compassionate.*"

"Never fear." She moved her hand downward, trailing her fingers over his well-muscled shoulders and across his chest. "Earlier you said you were falling in love with me. Sure and that's a two way street."

He laid a hand over hers, trapping it atop his hard, flat stomach. "Say it, *liebchen.*" He speared her with his smoky gaze. "If I could get the words out, anyone can."

She felt the words, tasted them on her tongue. Her cat purred deep inside, urging her on. "If wanting to spend my life with you, raise children with you, get up with you, and have you by my side every day for the rest of my life is love, then yes, I'm in love with you." Her throat thickened. "You're everything I've ever dreamed about."

"Thank you. I am ashamed to admit it, but I needed to hear you say just that."

"Why ashamed?"

A sheepish grin spread over his face. "Because big, tough espionage agents are not supposed to require such things." He snorted. "You should have watched the struggles Garen went through before he gave up and accepted he and Miranda were mates."

South of her hand, Lars' cock stirred to life. The tip grazed her, and she wriggled her hand from beneath his and curved her fingers around his growing erection. "Guess this little man didn't want to be left out of the conversation." She squeezed firmly, and his cock jumped in her hand.

Lars laughed. "He sees himself as a pretty important fellow."

She bent forward and ran her mouth down his breastbone and across his stomach. Just before she took him into her mouth, she looked up long enough to say, "Good, because I see him as pretty important too."

Tamara licked and kissed up and down the length of Lars' shaft.

His hips settled into a rhythm, and he thrust himself into the combination of mouth and hands she worked him with. Her nipples pebbled as lust electrified her nerves. Her pussy flooded, and the sensitive nub between her legs swelled with desire.

He pulled her upward until she knelt over him. Sliding forward, she seated him at the entrance to her body and pushed until he was all the way inside. He felt incredible, stretching her with his amazing cock. He was so big, he reached places no one else had ever come close to. She settled onto bent knees and watched his stern features melt into ecstasy as they made love.

Lars moved a hand between her legs and placed the other on a breast. He rubbed her clit in small, sensuous circles and twirled her nipple into a hard, aching point before moving to the other breast. Between his cock inside her and his fingers on her center of sensation, an orgasm spilled from her, racked her with delight, and left her gasping and panting above him.

"Perfect." He smiled up at her. "I wanted to watch you come."

It was what she'd wanted to do when she loved him with her tongue, but she'd been so hot her mind had turned to mush. He moved his hands to her hips and thrust deep, withdrew, and did it again. "This one will be for us," he said. "Touch yourself for me, like you did before."

She slid a hand between her legs, capturing her passion-slick nub. Something shifted and she felt him in her mind. Felt his body as if it were hers. Felt the heat of her around his cock. The added sensation was like a white-hot jolt of pure lust. She thrust hard against him, matching him stroke for stroke as they urged each other on.

When she came, she felt his orgasm deep in the pit of her belly and shrieked, almost beyond herself, drowning in sensation. There were no more boundaries. She was him. He was her. Joined body and soul forever.

She fell atop him, so shattered breathing took all her

concentration. When she could talk again, she asked. "What happened? What did you do?"

"It was not me, but us. When we made love as cats, it cemented the mate bond. We are truly one now, my darling, my love. You are mine, and I am yours for forever and a day."

"Sure and I love the sound of that," she murmured. "Forever and a day, *mo croi*, my heart. I will love you always."

Three months later
Heidelberg, Germany

LARS TWISTED from side to side, making certain his tuxedo didn't have any problems and that the studs and cufflinks were all in their proper holes. He caught a glimpse of his face in the mirror. He was smiling like a besotted fool. He'd have to do something about that, or he'd ruin his image for sure.

There was a lot to smile about, though. Tamara had taken to field agent training like a sculptor to a favored medium. She'd made such excellent progress, both he and Garen were positive she'd be ready for simple assignments before the end of the year.

The last three months had been little short of idyllic. They'd spent the first month with Garen and Miranda. Between field drills and physical conditioning during the day, intense, crazy lovemaking every night, and letting their cats out to romp and play, Lars was a happy man. He'd never been so fulfilled, heart, body, and soul. He'd wondered what sort of activities Tamara had chosen to stay in shape. It turned out she biked and ran, plus lifting weights. He'd added pilates and yoga, for concentration and balance, to her regimen, along with target practice.

In early May, they traveled to his home in Heidelberg, and he'd introduced her to Rubicon International's agents stationed in Europe. Though she'd had conversations with her family, she hadn't seen them. Lars had spoken with her father to formally request her hand in marriage. The other shifter grumbled, snarled, and told Lars flat out that if his daughter wasn't happy, he'd personally hunt him down and annihilate him. Both men had laughed after that, but Lars recognized truth when he heard it.

He was a bit nervous about meeting Tamara's family. All of them were coming for the wedding, even the brothers and sisters from her parents' earlier lives that she'd never met. While excited by the prospect of meeting more family, Tamara had disclosed that she felt apprehensive too. Everyone knew she'd avenged Moira's death, and she was uncertain if they'd laud her or tell her she'd been a fool.

Lars drew in a deep, appreciative breath. He'd have to get moving soon, but he could take a few moments more to daydream about his mate, soon to be his wife. Their relationship had deepened and blossomed. His cock stirred, but then it hardened whenever he thought about her. Beyond the sexual part of their relationship, though, they were well-matched. They both loved exercise and reading and watching old movies on late night television. When he'd admitted he was a closet opera buff, she'd clapped her hands together in delight, and they'd launched into a five hour conversation about various operas, with promises to see every single one over the next few years.

He'd moved well beyond falling in love to being in love. Deeply so. If that pseudo-cop hadn't pulled him over on his way to the airport and kept him cooling his heels, he'd never have met her. To have something so important reduced to chance chilled him, until he understood someone had been watching out for him that day. If shifters had a god, maybe he or she had taken pity on him, deciding he'd been alone long enough.

A sharp tap sounded on his door just before Garen tumbled into his room. He whistled long and low. "My but aren't we resplendent. Where'd you get the tux?"

"Back of my closet."

"Did you check it for moth holes?" Garen circled him like an overactive helicopter.

"Some of us keep mothballs in our armoires." He held out a hand. Garen clasped it. "Are the guests starting to arrive?"

Garen nodded. He clamped his jaw together, muttered, "What the hell," and drew Lars into a quick embrace. "I'm so happy for you." He clapped him on the back and withdrew a few steps.

"Thanks. Who would have guessed a year ago that before twelve months passed, we'd both be mated men?"

"Good point. Certainly not me. Are you ready?"

Lars nodded. He and Garen headed for the door at the same time, bumping shoulders before he motioned his oldest friend through ahead of him.

TAMARA WOVE LILY of the valley into her dark tresses with hands that only shook a little. She'd redone her makeup twice because tears had ruined it. She assessed her dress in the floor-length mirror. It truly was beautiful. Made of heirloom lace and silk, it had been in Lars' family for hundreds of years. Fine embroidery in pink, blue, and lilac covered the snug bodice. The gown had a dropped waist and hugged her figure from shoulder to hipline. Long, flowing sleeves of sheer silk fell to her wrists. The skirt draped in layers and ended in a train that was so long, she was afraid she'd trip over it in her high heels.

She flexed a foot and took a few tentative steps. Though she'd practiced walking in the shoes in the weeks since she bought them, they were still wretchedly uncomfortable.

"Can I come in?" Miranda called from the other side of the closed door.

"Please." Tamara turned and grinned at her friend as she slipped into the room. "By all the bloody saints, I'm nervous as a whore in church."

Miranda threw back her head and laughed. "You're funny. Do I look okay to be your matron of honor?"

Tamara glanced at the lavender linen suit, silk blouse, and sensible flat pumps. "You look gorgeous. Sure and I'd like to borrow your shoes."

"Eh, you can kick yours off right after the ceremony. I'm so damned tall. If I wore heels, I'd tower over Garen."

"He wouldn't care. I've never seen a man more in love, except maybe Lars."

Miranda snorted. "I know he wouldn't, but I would. Christ! I've felt like an overgrown moose my whole life. I hit six feet in something like seventh grade. I was taller than everyone—boys too —for years."

She plucked pins from Tamara's nerveless fingers and went to work on her hair, weaving more flowers into it. "I've never seen Lars so happy. I swear, he's like a new man. Watching the two of you together has damn near brought me to tears a couple of times, and I don't cry easily."

Tamara smiled softly. "Don't. I cry at the drop of a hat. Sure and I don't want to start all over on my makeup—again." She met her friend's gaze in the mirror. "It has been good. Amazingly so. I never thought I'd fall head over heels in love and have every day just get better and better. It's not that we don't have our moments, but he listens to me. And I listen to him. If we can't agree, we work together to find common ground."

"Being able to talk is important. Garen and I had hellacious arguments in the beginning, but they've thinned out. There." She handed Tamara a mirror. "What do you think?"

Tamara turned slowly, holding the glass so she could see the back of her hair. "It's wonderful. Were you a hair stylist in a former life?"

"Nope. I didn't even have any girlfriends to trade 'dos' with in high school. Once I shifted, and my aunt made me feel like shit about it, I kept to myself."

Tamara's heart hurt for her friend. Miranda had told her about the *dirty, fucking shifter* epithets her aunt hurled at her. At least the woman hadn't turned her in, but Miranda grew up feeling seriously flawed. It was one reason she'd gone into the Green Berets: to prove her mettle, while she hid from the world.

She wrapped her arms around Miranda. "Sure and my family will love you." Tamara straightened. "Speaking of which, let's go. I want to get the hugs and kisses with Mum and Da over with before the ceremony. Och, sure and I'll never get through it without dissolving into tears."

"Of course you will." Miranda winked. "Be prepared, though. I saw Lars before I came in here." She whistled. "Wow! What a knockout that man is in formal clothes. If I wasn't madly in love with Garen, I swear I'd give you a run for your money."

Tamara laughed and walked out into the hall. She looped her train around her wrist to keep it out of the way before she tackled the stairs. Lars may have said he lived in a manor house, but it was more like a castle. Ten thousand square feet of marble, leaded crystal, granite, and stone sat atop a hill, surrounded by stables, servants' quarters, and other outbuildings. It had taken her weeks to find her way around, and she still hadn't seen either attic or basement. The place was furnished with priceless antiques and thick, Aubusson rugs. Lars assured her he'd bought everything new. His things became antiques by dint of enough time passing.

Halfway down the staircase, her parents' voices drifted up to her. Tamara tottered down the rest of the way as fast as she could. "Mum? Da?" she cried.

"Right here, sweetheart." Her da, a huge, strongly muscled man with coal black hair and green eyes, strode toward her and crushed her against him. "Sure and 'tis good to see you again, princess." He was dressed as formally as she'd ever seen him in a crisp, black suit, an off-white shirt, and a maroon tie.

Tamara didn't trust herself to speak. She clung to her father, filled with love for the man who'd raised her to believe in herself. It could've been so much worse. She might have had dead parents and a bigoted aunt like Miranda's.

Her mum closed on them in a rustle of pale green long silk skirts with a hip-length ivory tunic atop them. Her red-blonde hair was braided in an intricate pattern. Blue eyes, exactly like Tamara's, glowed with pride. "'Tis a beautiful bride you are, darlin'."

"Och, thanks, Mum. Sure and I've missed the two of you."

"How about me?" Her brother, Devon, flanked by her other three brothers, crowded close.

She shot him a mock frown. "Maybe not you so much."

"Little sisters always were a pain in the arse," he declared just before he wormed between her and their da to draw her into a hug.

Tamara caught a flicker of movement out of the corner of one eye. She disengaged herself from her brother's arms and turned to face Lars and Garen. "Sure and it's bad luck for you to see me before the wedding."

"I will take my chances." Lars grasped both her hands in his and bent to kiss her cheek. "You are so beautiful. I have to be the luckiest man alive."

"Just so long as you always remember that and treat her like a queen, we'll have no truck with one another." Christian MacBride offered his hand. Letting go of Tamara, Lars gripped it.

"Nice to meet you, sir." He half bowed over their clasped hands.

Christian cocked his head to one side. "One of the old ones, aren't you? I'd known, but forgotten." He bowed in return. When he straightened, he said, "Perhaps we can catch a wee bit of time after the ceremony to get to know one another better."

"I would like that." Lars hesitated. "It is probably safe enough for us to visit Ireland. I was waiting to see…"

"No need to say anything further." Christian jumped into the breach when Lars' words trailed off. He motioned to Tamara. "Come with me. There are quite a few family members who'd dearly love to meet you."

"Sure and she'll be with you in just a moment." Leona took her daughter's arm and led her a few feet away. "Thanks be to you, darlin'," she whispered low, "I'll be havin' my family whole again. Your da was so afraid if the lot of us gathered, someone would figure out what we were."

"There's still that risk," Tamara whispered back, concern tugging at her midsection.

"Aye, but Christian was willin' to let the chips fall. After losing poor Moira, he wanted everyone together for your weddin'."

Tamara kissed her mother's cheek, inhaling her familiar, soothing fragrance. "I love you, Mum."

"Aw, darlin', my darlin' daughter, not near so much as I love you. Get on wi' you now. We can throw cake at each other after the ceremony."

"Och, a fine old Irish tradition."

Her mother grinned. "That it is."

Tamara glanced toward where her father stood, surrounded by at least twenty others, maybe a few more.

Sure and those must be all my brothers and sisters.

She hurried to his side, anxious to meet each and every one of them.

Lars stepped out onto one of many terraces leading from the second floor ballroom of his home and gazed at the mix of antique and modern that was Heidelberg. The ancient German city had never looked so beautiful to him. The night was warm and clear, an idyllic summer evening for a perfect wedding. The actual ceremony had been brief, performed by a magistrate. Nonetheless, the words had etched into his soul. He would honor, protect, and love Tamara to the end of their days.

"And beyond if I have anything to say about it," he murmured.

"What was that, my love?" Tamara floated to his side. Swathed in his great-grandmother's gown, she was unbelievably striking. The dress had needed serious alterations, since Tamara was much taller than women from earlier times, but the seamstress had a deft hand, and the gown looked as if it had been made for her.

He smiled. "I was taking a breather from our guests."

"Me too." She laughed, and the sound resonated in his soul. "Neither of us are exactly social butterfly types. I adore my family, but I looked around and didn't see you, so I came a'hunting."

"You can hunt me down anytime you want."

"Truly?"

"Of course. We are mated, and married. It makes me eminently hunt-able."

"Do you suppose we might live here for a while?"

Something lay beneath her words, maybe longing for the home she was certain she'd lost forever. He placed his hands on her shoulders. "What would please you?"

She drew her brows together. He'd come to recognize her expressions and knew she was taking her time because he'd asked an important question. "I want to stay here and maybe have a country house in Ireland too." She grinned impishly. "Sure and then when we wanted to get away from this side of the Atlantic, we could visit Garen and Miranda. Och, what else?" Her eyes twinkled up at him. "You could be teaching me how to fly one of the bigger planes. I thought to mention it before—"

"It is not as if we have had large chunks of spare time. Everything you want is not only possible, but easily done."

"You wouldn't mind being close to Da and Mum a few weeks of the year? And all those brand new family members we just met."

"I respect your father. He and I have much to talk about. He has not made a firm decision, but he may return to working for us, particularly since you are part of our operation now." Lars snorted. "Somehow, I suspect he wants to keep a close eye on you, and determine for himself just how trustworthy I am."

"Ooooh." She clapped a hand over her mouth. "That would be wonderful. Not the *keeping an eye* part, but working together. Da is solid. Nothing rattles him."

"*Ja.* Garen said as much." Lars was reluctant to break the mood, but he felt compelled to say, "The work we do is dangerous. Do not forget that part. It is why your father changed careers. Your mother worried herself sick every time he left the house."

"Dangerous, yes. Sure and it adds a fine edge to living, though. I haven't felt this alive—ever." She nodded thoughtfully. "For Mum and Da, I'm guessing they'll work things out." She twirled away from him, her skirts billowing, and then waltzed back. When she stopped, she was only inches away. "I'm happy," she said breathlessly. "So happy it scares me."

He nodded, feeling suddenly solemn. "I meant every word of our vows, *liebchen*. Now and always."

She melted into his arms and twined hers around him. "I haven't forgotten what you said in bed that night. You told me you'd love me forever and a day, sure and that was when I knew in my heart of hearts I'd marry you."

"*Ja, liebchen,* my beloved. I will love you so long as there is breath in my body. When there is not, I will love you still. If that is not forever, I do not know what is."

She tilted her head back. He closed his mouth over hers. The kiss was tender, sweet, filled with the love coursing through him.

"Och, so that's where they are." Christian's voice boomed. "None of that, you two. You'll have all your lives to moon over each other."

"Your da's right, darlin'." Leona marched to where they stood. "Just now you've guests to attend to."

Lars straightened and turned Tamara in his arms so she stood by his side. "You heard your kinfolk." His tone was stern, but he was smiling. "Looks as if we have been remiss."

"That you have." Christian fell in next to Lars as the four of them walked back inside the house. "'Tisn't every day I get a brand new son-in-law. We have toasts to drink, food to share, and tall tales to spin."

"It is not every day I become part of something this special." Lars beamed. Gratitude swelled in his chest. "Thank you."

Christian turned. "For what?"

"The gift of your daughter and the rest of your family." He met the other man's gaze. "I was alone for far too long."

"Sure and you'll never be alone again." Christian clapped him on the back.

Leona handed him a glass of champagne and said, "To a long and happy life."

"I'll drink to that." Tamara grinned and picked up a champagne glass of her own.

"*Ja.* To a long and happy life for us all." Lars lifted the delicate Waterford crystal flute to his lips and drank.

This is the end of *Lars*. Other Rubicon International books will be forthcoming, but for now Lars and Garen have closed important chapters in their lives. Both are mated, and RI will continue as a force to be reckoned with.

ABOUT THE AUTHOR

Ann Gimpel is a national bestselling author. A lifelong aficionado of the unusual, she began writing speculative fiction a few years ago. Since then her short fiction has appeared in a number of webzines and anthologies. Her longer books run the gamut from urban fantasy to paranormal romance. Once upon a time, she nurtured clients, now she nurtures dark, gritty fantasy stories that push hard against reality. When she's not writing, she's in the backcountry getting down and dirty with her camera. She's published over 50 books to date, with several more planned for 2018 and beyond. A husband, grown children, grandchildren and wolf hybrids round out her family.

Keep up with her at 8www.anngimpel.com or http://anngimpel.blogspot.com

If you enjoyed what you read, get in line for special offers and pre-release special reads. Sign up for Ann's newsletter on her website or her blog.

BOOK DESCRIPTION: WINNING GLORY

If you enjoyed the Rubicon books, you might also like GenTech Rebellion, another action adventure romance series. A sample from *Winning Glory*, first book in that series, follows.

After years as a black ops CIA agent, nothing surprises Roy Kincaid, yet his current assignment is close to a bust. How could his target—renegade genetic freaks—drop off the radar as if they never existed? Burnt out and discouraged, he hunches over a meal in a backwater diner when a half-frozen woman with the look of an abused runaway staggers through the door. On his feet in an instant, Roy kicks himself. His first instinct is to help her, make certain she stays long enough for the bluish cast to leave her lips. His second is to finish his meal and leave. The world is full of broken women. It's not his job to fix them, but he can't take his eyes off her.

Glory's telepathic ability blares a harsh warning. Roy hunts those like her, but damn if he didn't buy her dinner. Maybe she can fool him, just for tonight. Add a dry motel room to the meal. If she plays it very cool, he'll never find out she's on the run from the same group he's targeted for death.

Enhanced genetics only go so far. A roadblock and her face on a *Most Wanted* flyer shatter her fragile truce with Roy. If her Handlers find her, they'll kill her. If Roy finds out what she is, she'll be worse than dead.

Series Backstory:

Sometime between the interminable wars in the Middle East and 9/11, the United States moved forward breeding a race of super humans. Clandestine labs formed, armed with eager scientists who'd always yearned to manipulate human DNA. At first the clones looked promising, growing to fighting size in as little as a dozen years, but V1 had design flaws.

Seven years ago, a rogue group turned on their creators, blew up the lab, and hit all the other breeding farms, freeing whomever they could find. In the intervening time, they've retreated to hidden compounds and created a society run by men. Women are kept on a tight leash because the men fear if they discover their innate power, they'd launch their own rebellion.

WINNING GLORY, CHAPTER ONE

Shadows surrounded Glory. The darkness provided some shielding, but she wanted more—lots more. Too bad invisibility wasn't an option. Her pulse thudded against her eardrums. Sweat formed a banner across her forehead and dripped into her eyes. They stung, and she cursed her human genetic base. When she'd been designed, why the hell hadn't they deep-sixed the annoying things like sweat and fear?

"Get moving!" Her Handler's voice pounded through her head, projected telepathically.

She started. In the midst of her ambivalence, she'd forgotten about the Handlers—also called Nameless Ones—lurking just outside her work area. This was her first real assignment, and they didn't trust her by herself. She blew out a wry breath. They'd probably never trust her, but she was useful.

A low growl followed the Handler's terse words. She scowled as the noise scraped across her preternaturally sharp senses. Glory wanted to balk, make a break for freedom, but it'd be pointless. They'd be on her so fast, she'd be lucky to buy herself an hour.

She gazed straight ahead, assessing her objective. The large office building in downtown Seattle's business district wasn't as deserted as she'd hoped. Lights shone from about a quarter of its windows. If she were fortunate, her target would be unoccupied, but she knew what to say if it wasn't.

No, I know what to do... Talking wasn't exactly on the table.

She sucked in a ragged breath, blew it out, and did it again. Her hair was pulled into a bun, its weight heavy on her neck, but at least it wouldn't come loose and obscure her vision if she had to move quickly.

The growl came again, and she shot forward, trying to walk as if she had every right to be on Pine Street at eleven at night. Unfamiliar high heels lent her an awkward rolling gait, and she pulled her skirt a little higher, so she could adjust her stride. When she'd complained about the black wool business suit and heels, she'd been told she had to look the part if she ran into anyone. She'd have practiced walking in the unfamiliar shoes, but the entire outfit had materialized—dropped in her dorm by a Handler—half an hour before she left her compound.

She fumbled a key card from her suit pocket with damp fingers and swiped it through a reader next to huge, double glass doors that opened onto a lavishly furnished lobby. Pink, white, and purple orchids, plush leather furniture, and glistening gray marble floors felt overwhelming after her spartan existence. After a pause that felt far too long, the scanner's red lights shifted to green, and the door's locking mechanism snicked softly.

Glory darted forward and felt a rush of air as the door swooshed shut behind her. She'd have to use the card to get out too, so she glanced sidelong to identify the reader's location on the lobby side. For long moments, she didn't see a thing, and her already rapid heart rate escalated, making her dizzy.

Doesn't matter. Head for the elevators. I can turn and look better from there.

A creaky grating stopped her cold, until an older, dark-skinned man dressed in a navy blue uniform came into view. He pushed a wheeled bucket with a mop sticking out of it. "Evening, ma'am." He dipped his chin toward her. "Late to be working, isn't it?"

She nodded. "I, uh, I forgot something I needed."

He nodded back. "Always something, eh?" His smile displayed several missing teeth; grizzled gray hair lay flat against his head.

Because she was too keyed up to talk, and finding words was hard, she trotted toward the elevator, nearly twisting an ankle in the process from her sleek, black pumps. She still had the electronic card in hand. The Nameless Ones had done reconnaissance and funneled needed data into her processing unit. It was how she knew she'd need the key card to call the elevator after hours—and everything else about this assignment.

She swiped the card and pushed the up button. Somewhere above her, machinery whirred. She wanted to look back at the front door, but self-preservation and not attracting attention trumped everything.

The housekeeper whistled as he drew his mop across the shiny floor. She listened, trying to make out the tune, but it wasn't familiar. The elevator doors opened, and she stepped inside, turning as she did to catch a glimpse of the electronic scanner that had to be near the front door.

Breath rattled from her constricted lungs. There it was. About a foot to the right of the door, which was why she hadn't noticed it before. Excellent. Her egress—assuming she made it that far— would be smooth, rather than awkward. It'd look suspicious if she had no idea how to exit the building. Floors whooshed past, and she got out on the fourteenth. Squaring her shoulders, she took advantage of her almost six-foot height to project the illusion she belonged here, in the center of corporate America late at night.

This building in the heart of Seattle was as close to the Silicon Valley as the Northwest got. Many major hardware and software manufacturers had offices here, but she was only focused on one of them—Dynamic Solutions. DS was deeply involved in government contracting for classified genetic research. The Handlers told her that much, but nothing further, and she'd known better than to ask.

Her heels beat a staccato on green-veined, creamy marble as she made her way to the end of the hall. She traded the key card still clutched in her sweaty hand for a different one, swiped it, and slipped on transparent latex gloves before letting herself into a mercifully dark suite of offices.

Get what I came for and leave, ran through her mind like a mantra. The cleanup person had seen her, but he wouldn't be a problem, not so long as everything else went smoothly. Her heart still beat too fast, and she was sweating despite the cool November evening and the sixty degree temperature in the building, but so far so good.

The office layout was exactly what she'd seen in schematics. She strode purposively toward a corner office. The door was shut and she twisted the latch.

It didn't turn.

Goddammit! Locked. What do I do now? A perverse part of her thrilled because the Nameless Ones' intel had flaws. She hated them so much, any evidence of their weakness meant maybe she could escape someday.

Her practical side intruded, and she looked for a keycard slot in the door. Picking locks was easy; it wouldn't slow her down much. When she didn't find one, she hunted for an electronic device and groaned when she saw a retinal scanner. She could defeat it, but she needed permission to break protocol, plus she didn't want to kick off the building's alarm system if there was a way around it.

"There's a retinal scanner," she sent telepathically to her Handlers.

"Break the lock."

"But that will set off alarms," she protested. Her thin, silk blouse stuck to her, and she pulled it away from her breasts, hoping to dry her damp skin.

"Give us credit for something," the voice snarled. *"We disabled them.*

Hurry. We don't have all night." After a pause, he added, *"Speed is your friend."*

Glory stared at the door. She could open the lock with her mind. It wouldn't be hard. Had the Nameless One lied to her about the alarms? They certainly weren't beyond that, but if she couldn't believe them, it made every shred of intel supporting this mission suspect. She closed her teeth over her bottom lip so hard she tasted blood. She had to do something. Fish or cut bait.

If she left empty handed, there'd be hell to pay. Time in a cell to contemplate her failure. She shook herself to force her body into action. It had been a long road to get where she was right now, earning enough of the Nameless Ones' trust to be allowed out of the compound. She might never regain the ground she lost if she jack-rabbited out of here with her tail between her legs.

Fuck it.

She called the power that flowed through her mind. Electricity crackled from her fingertips, forcing the retinal scanner's hand, and the door sprang open. Doubts that had dogged her ever since she stood outside plotting her course of action vanished. She vaulted through the door, kicked it shut, and dove into a black leather chair sitting behind an enormous mahogany desk. She flipped switches, activating the computer and movie-sized flat screen monitor.

"Come on," she urged under her breath, fingers poised over a keyboard. A box flashed onto the screen requesting username and password information. She typed what she'd been told—and got an error message. Glory typed it again. Same message.

What the hell?

One explanation jumped to the top of the heap. The computer's owner must have changed it after the Nameless Ones infiltrated this company. She didn't hesitate. Assuming the username would be the same, she typed it and then created anagrams from the password in every permutation and combination. The process was quick, because her brain was just like the computer she was hacking into.

With her fingers moving so fast they were a blur, she blended her consciousness with the CPU droning at her feet. When it wanted to shut down and sound an alarm after three tries to access its secrets, she reached deep enough into its operating system code to stymie the automatic rejection sequence and bypass the password entirely.

"Yes!" Glory fist pumped the air when menus rolled across the screen. She yanked a flash drive from her skirt pocket, slotted it into a USB port, and started the download, selecting files as she went. She covered her electronic presence so well that if she wasn't disturbed, no one would ever know she'd been here. The company had safeguards to keep her from breaking in from an external computer, but they couldn't keep her out when she was logged in from one of their own.

She wondered how the Nameless Ones acquired the username and worthless password, but they never told her things like that. They'd probably borrowed data from one of those software programs where the unwary store all their important data—never realizing how easy they are to hack. Or installed a keystroke logger. She smiled wryly. What a bunch of rubes humans were. If she ever escaped the Nameless Ones, blending in shouldn't be too hard.

When the drive filled, she inserted another and then two more.

Her fingers skimmed the keyboard as file after file dropped into her drives. Only one more drive and she'd be done. There. Glory pocketed her flash drives, four in all, and shut the machine down. She'd just gotten up from the chair when she heard the outer office door open. Thank Christ she hadn't turned on any lights. Floor to ceiling curtains partially shrouded windows that looked out on a busy waterfront. She raced behind one and arranged it to hide her.

Barely breathing, she waited, shifting from foot to foot. Glory rode herd on her nerves and forced stillness, concentrating hard to alter reality. It wasn't a skill she was good at since the Handlers didn't encourage its use.

Fuck! Go away so I can leave.

An unpleasant whirring clawed at her sensitive hearing as the retinal scanner did its work and allowed access to whoever was standing outside. So much for altering reality to suit her needs.

"I'll just be a minute," a man's voice spoke, and he clumped through the door.

"Work, work, work," a woman groused. "You promised tonight would be just us, and here we are back at your goddamned office."

The heavy footsteps paused. "This *goddamned office* supports you," the man said, his tone heavy with bitterness.

Clearly, this was an old bone of contention between the couple. While she'd never lived around humans, Glory watched plenty of television, and she spent hours each day on the Internet.

She took shallow breaths. Her nose tickled, but she pinched it to avoid sneezing. It didn't look as if the man and his partner would be here long. The footsteps started again and then stopped.

"That's odd," the man said.

Glory's heart jumped into hyper drive. What hadn't she done? Was it the chair? Had she left it wrong, somehow? Who the fuck recalled exactly how they left their chair anyway?

"What's odd?" Lighter steps, wearing heels.

"I always push my chair in when I leave. It's been moved."

"Oh for Christ's sake, Lloyd. That high-clearance cleaning staff you were going on about the other day must've moved it. Let's go."

"Mmph. You're probably right."

A desk drawer opened and closed, followed by another. More steps as the couple left, door shutting behind them.

Glory didn't breathe normally until the door closed. She counted to five hundred very slowly before she left her hiding place and exited the office. Even though it should be enough time, she remained frightened she'd run into Lloyd and his grumpy companion. Once she was in the corridor leading to the elevator at the end of the fourteenth floor, she started to relax.

I did it.

Not yet. I'm not out yet.

She rode the elevator down and made her way to the outside door. The janitor was nowhere in sight, and the door's scanner flashed green as soon as she swiped her key card. The chill damp of a Seattle night felt like a balm on her overheated skin, and she walked briskly toward the pickup point two blocks away. The shoes didn't bother her as much. Maybe she was getting used to them.

Nothing could go wrong now. She was in the clear. She had what she came for. Glory snaked a hand into her pocket and cradled the drives. She'd memorized the file names driving here, but they were in some kind of code that didn't make sense, even when she ran it through her augmented brain. She'd been instructed not to take time to read any of what she'd stolen. Good thing she didn't break protocol. As it was, she escaped detection by a very narrow margin. A few more seconds downloading, and Lloyd would've caught her in the act.

Breath hissed through her teeth, and her stomach clenched. If Lloyd had waltzed in before she shut the computer off, he'd have turned his office upside down hunting for an intruder, given how spun out he was about his fucking chair. She shook her head. Her instructions were to kill if she were apprehended. A quick blast to melt neurons into mush. Not that she hadn't practiced with dummies, but she'd never actually harmed a living creature. When it got right down to it, she wasn't certain she could.

"It's about time." A man dressed in black sidled next to her from the maw of a nearby alleyway.

"Did you get it?" A second man, similarly dressed, joined the first. Both were tall, close to six feet four, with shaggy dark hair and heavily muscled bodies. They always wore dark glasses, even indoors, so she had no idea what their eyes looked like. The men were genetically altered, just like her. One of the government's many experiments that had leaped its boundaries, gone sideways, and produced freaks that had to be hidden away from polite society.

The thought brought a smile to her lips, and the second man

slugged her in the arm. "Look at her. Grinning like a shit-eating demon. Of course she got it."

"Almost didn't," she said. "The man who works in that office came back."

The first man turned her head toward her and furled his brows. "And?"

"I didn't have to do anything. I hid behind a curtain until he left."

"Excellent." The man blew out a tense breath.

"Yeah," the other man seconded. "Always better when we don't have to send in the drones to clean up."

Glory hurried to keep up with them. She'd never heard this part before. "So someone would have shown up to get rid of the bodies?"

"Ssht!" One of the Nameless Ones jabbed her hard with his elbow.

It felt like a steel pipe pounding into her side, and she grunted with pain but understood to keep her mouth shut. They came to a black SUV, and she got into the back seat, rubbing her sore ribs. The men climbed in the front, and the vehicle pulled away from the curb at a sedate pace.

She twisted around and got onto her knees, so she could reach her bundle of clothes behind the rear seat. Once she had them, she faced forward again and dug for her worn black trousers and battered lace up boots. Realizing she still had the clear, latex gloves on, she peeled them off and asked, "Is it okay if I change into my other clothes?" She kicked off the high heels before getting an answer.

"Permission granted." The Nameless One in the passenger seat adjusted the rear view mirror so his gaze met hers. "Mind if I watch?"

It wasn't a question. Not really, so she didn't bother to answer, just pulled on her pants before she slithered out of her skirt. She was damned if she'd give him any more of a peep show than she had to. Because he'd want to humor her, and maybe catch a glimpse of tit, she gathered her courage. "You never answered me about the bodies."

"That's because you asked in a public place." He sounded annoyingly patronizing. "Come on, babe. Aren't you going to take that jacket off? And your blouse?"

She shrugged the jacket off and undid one button, but very slowly. Feeling like she might have the upper hand for once, albeit temporarily, she crooked two fingers and smiled. "Information first."

"You drive a hard bargain." He reached a hand toward his lap. "That's not all that's hard."

The driver shot a glance at his partner. "She's off limits, and you know it."

"Who'd tell?"

"I would," the driver said sourly. He twisted the rear view mirror and looked at her. "We never leave evidence of our missions. If you'd had to terminate anyone, we would've done away with the bodies, and any associated untidiness."

"Thank you for the information." Glory pulled a bulky gray, wool sweater out of her clothes bag and put it on over her cream-colored silk blouse. Because her head ached from the weight of her hair, she pulled the pins holding her bun in place and sheaves of shiny darkness rippled around her.

"Aw, what happened to my tit show?" The Nameless One sounded annoyed.

"It was cancelled." Glory leaned back against the leather seat and exhaled long and loud.

The man in the passenger seat moved so fast, she didn't understand how he could possibly have vaulted over the divider and be seated next to her. The chiseled lines of his face were set into a harsh expression, and he shoved a hand in front of her.

"Give." He opened and closed his fist.

Understanding, she dug into the clothes bag and found the skirt she'd just removed. Glory extracted the flash drives and handed them over. "You can go back to the front seat," she told him.

"Nah, think I'll stay right where I am." He leered at her and patted his lap again.

"I still don't understand why you didn't have me merge with the computer and do a direct download into my brain," she said. "It'd have been much faster." A flash of insight slammed her between the eyes. She could've done both—if she weren't so scared of her Handlers.

"Too much temptation." The man eyed her. "This way, we know you didn't peek."

She smelled his arousal, and it disgusted her. All the Nameless Ones disgusted her. The driver was correct about her being off limits. They left her alone for some unknown reason—or they had until now. Her and the other girls like her. Glory closed her eyes to block out the man next to her. She could still smell him, but at least she didn't have to look at him.

She let her body sag against the seat. It was a long drive back to the compound, well over two hours. Maybe she could catch some sleep. She felt hungry, but asking them to stop at a fast food joint would buy her bupkis. A bottle of water rattled in the door; she made a grab for it, unscrewed the cap, and drained it. At least the Nameless One was keeping his distance. Good. They'd never pawed her before, but there was always a first time.

As miles clicked by, she scrolled what she knew about her origins through her mind. It wasn't much, which was frustrating. It felt as if there was a locked file in her head, just out of reach. If she could only pop the code, everything would become clear.

Yeah, I've been trying to decipher that secret for years.

Sometimes, she got tantalizingly close, only to have truth fritter away in puffs of smoke.

"You'll never figure it out," the man sitting next to her said.

"Gawk! Stay out of my head." She drew as far away from him as she could, hugging the door panel.

"I can't fuck you, but no one said I couldn't rape your thoughts," the man retorted smugly.

Glory ignored him. She withdrew deep into the place in her mind no one could reach and hovered there. Did the ignorant asshole next to her know she could kill him from where she sat without even touching him?

An unpleasant thought intruded. Of course he knew, because he could do the same thing.